America's Most Unusual Writer

This fascinating volume is devoted to the work of one of the most dynamic, controversial and unusual living American writers—Henry Miller, author of such bold and vital books as *Tropic of Cancer* and *Tropic of Capricorn.*

Miller's frank and original expression of the most intimate thoughts and feelings of men and women, his unique style of writing and his acute observations on modern civilization have brought him international fame. Among the many eminent writers and critics who praise his work are T. S. Eliot, George Orwell, John Dos Passos, Aldous Huxley, Edmund Wilson, and H. L. Mencken.

All who enjoy and appreciate good writing will find this brilliant collection of Miller's stories a new and unforgettable reading experience.

"His is one of the most beautiful styles today."
                                        —*H. L. Mencken*

" . . . a literary live wire."—*St. Louis Post Dispatch*

"Mr. Miller's love goes out to the little people, men whom the world has never noticed."
                                        —*Nashville Tennessean*

Henry Miller

NIGHTS OF LOVE
AND
LAUGHTER

With an Introduction by Kenneth Rexroth

A SIGNET BOOK

Published by **THE NEW AMERICAN LIBRARY**

*Published as a SIGNET BOOK
By Arrangement with New Directions*

FIRST PRINTING, NOVEMBER, 1955
SECOND PRINTING, JUNE, 1960

Library of Congress Catalog Card No. 55-11641

*SIGNET BOOKS are published by
The New American Library of World Literature, Inc.
501 Madison Avenue, New York 22, New York*

PRINTED IN THE UNITED STATES OF AMERICA

Contents

Introduction

It is a wonderful thing that some of Henry Miller's work at last is coming out in a popular edition in the United States. Henry Miller is a really popular writer, a writer of and for real people, who, in other countries, is read, not just by highbrows, or just by the wider public which reads novels, but by common people, by the people who, in the United States, read comic books. As the Southern mountain woman said of her hero son, dead in Korea, "Mister, he was sure a great reader, always settin' in the corner with a piece of cold bread and one of them funny books." In Czech, Hindustani, and Japanese, this is the bulk of Miller's public. In the United States he has been kept away from a popular public and his great novels have been banned; therefore only highbrows who could import them from France have read him.

I once crossed the Atlantic—eighteen days in a Compagnie Générale Transatlantique freighter—with a cabin mate, a French African Negro, who was only partially literate, but who was able to talk for hours on the comparative merits of *Black Spring* and the *Tropic of Cancer* and the *Tropic of Capricorn*. When he found out I came from California and knew Miller, he started treating me as if I were an archangel newly descended, and never tired of questions about *le Beeg Sur* and *les camarades de M'sieu Millaire*. He had a mental picture of poor Henry living on a mountaintop, surrounded by devoted handmaids and a bevy of zoot-suited existentialist jitterbugs.

This picture, I have discovered, is quite commonly believed in by people who should have better sense. Miners in the Pyrenees, camel drivers in Tlemcen, gondoliers in

Venice, and certainly every *poule* in Paris, when they hear you're from California, ask, first thing, in one voice, "Do you know *M'sieu Millaire?*" This doesn't mean he isn't read by the intellectuals, the cultured people over there. He is. In fact, I should say he has become part of the standard repertory of reading matter everywhere but in England and the United States. If you have read Balzac, or Baudelaire, or Goethe, you are also expected to have read Miller. He is certainly one of the most widely read American writers, along with Upton Sinclair, Jack London, Fenimore Cooper, William Faulkner and Erskine Caldwell.

This is the way it should be. Nothing was sadder than the "proletarian novelist" of a few years back, the product of a sociology course and a subscription to a butcher-paper weekly, eked out with a terrified visit to a beer parlor on the other side of the tracks and a hasty scurry past a picket line. Nobody read him but other Greenwich Village aesthetes like himself. The people Henry Miller writes about read him. They read him because he gives them something they cannot find elsewhere in print. It may not be precisely the real world, but it is nearer to it than most other writing, and it is certainly nearer than most so-called realistic writing.

Once the written word was the privilege of priests and priestly scribes. Although thousands of years have passed, vestiges of that special privilege and caste artificiality still cling to it. It has been said that literature is a class phenomenon. Can you remember when you first started to read? Doubtless you thought that some day you would find in books the truth, the answer to the very puzzling life you were discovering around you. But you never did. If you were alert, you discovered that books were conventions, as unlike life as a game of chess. The written word is a sieve. Only so much of reality gets through as fits the size and shape of the screen, and in some ways that is never enough. This is only partly due to the necessary conventions of speech, writing, communication generally. Partly it is due to the structure of language. With us in our Western European civilization this takes the form of Indo-European grammar crystallized in what we call Aristotelian logic. But most of the real difficulty of communication comes from social convention, from a vast conspiracy to agree to accept the world as something it really isn't at all. Even the realistic novels of a writer like Zola are not much closer to the real thing than the documents written in Egyptian hieroglyphics. They are just a different, most complex, distortion.

Literature is a social defense mechanism. Remember again when you were a child. You thought that some day you would grow up and find a world of real adults—the people who really made things run—and understood how and why things ran. People like the Martian aristocrats in science fiction. Your father and mother were pretty silly, and the other grownups were even worse—but somewhere, some day, you'd find the real grownups and possibly even be admitted to their ranks. Then, as the years went on, you learned, through more or less bitter experience, that there aren't, and never have been, any such people, anywhere. Life is just a mess, full of tall children, grown stupider, less alert and resilient, and nobody knows what makes it go—as a whole, or any part of it. *But nobody ever tells*.

Henry Miller tells. Anderson told *about* the little boy and the Emperor's new clothes. Miller is the little boy himself. He tells about the Emperor, about the pimples on his behind, and the warts on his private parts, and the dirt between his toes. Other writers in the past have done this, of course, and they are the great ones, the real classics. But they have done it within the conventions of literature. They have used the forms of the Great Lie to expose the truth. Some of this literature is comic, with a terrifying laughter— Cervantes' *Don Quixote,* Jonson's *Volpone,* Machiavelli's *Mandragola,* Shakespeare's *King Lear*. Some of it is tragic, in the ordinary sense, like the *Iliad* or Thucydides' history, or *Macbeth*. In the last analysis it is all tragic, even Rabelais, because life itself is tragic. With very few exceptions, however, it is all conventional. It disguises itself in the garments of harmless artistic literature. It sneaks in and betrays the complacent and deluded. A great work of art is a kind of Trojan Horse. There are those who believe that this is all there is to the art of poetry—sugar-coating the pills of prussic acid with which the poet doses the Enemy.

It is hard to tell sometimes when Miller is being ironic and when he is being naive. He is the master of a deadpan style, just as he has a public personality that alternates between quiet gentleness—"like a dentist," he describes it— and a sort of deadpan buffoonery. This has led some critics to consider him a naive writer, a "modern primitive," like the painter Rousseau. In a sense this is true.

Miller is a very unliterary writer. He writes as if he had just invented the alphabet. When he writes about a book, he writes as if he were the first and only man who had ever read it—and, furthermore, as if it weren't a book but a piece of the living meat whacked off Balzac or Rimbaud or whoever. Rousseau was one of the finest painters of modern times. But he was absolutely impervious to the ordinary devices of his craft. This was not because he was not exposed to other artists. He spent hours every week in the Louvre and he was, from the 1880s to the eve of the First World War, the intimate of all the best painters and writers, the leading intellectuals of Paris. It didn't make any difference. He just went his way, being Henri Rousseau, a very great artist. But when he talked or wrote, he spouted terrible nonsense. He wasn't just a crank, but quite off his rocker in an amiable sort of way. This is not true of Miller.

In some mysterious way, Miller has preserved an innocence of the practice of Literature-with-a-capital-L which is almost unique in history. Likewise he has preserved an innocence of heart. But he is not unsophisticated. In the first place, he writes a muscular, active prose in which something is always going on and which is always under control. True, he often rambles and gets windy, but only because he likes to ramble and hear his head roar. When he wants to tell you something straight from the shoulder, he makes you reel.

Now the writer most like Miller in some ways, the eighteenth-century naïf, Restif de la Bretonne, is certainly direct from the innocent heart, but he can be as tedious as a year's mail of a Lonely Hearts Club, with the same terrible verisimilitude of a "Mature woman, broadminded, likes books and music" writing to "Bachelor, fifty-two, steady job, interested in finer things." And, in addition, Restif is full of arrant nonsense, every variety of crackpot notion. If you want the common man of the eighteenth century, with his heart laid bare, you will find him in Restif. But you will also find thousands of pages of sheer boredom, and hundreds of pages of quite loony and obviously invented pornography. Miller too is likely at times to go off the deep end about the lost continent of Mu or astrology or the "occult," but it is for a different reason. If the whole shebang is a lie anyway,

certainly the amusing lies, the lies of the charlatans who
have never been able to get the guillotine in their hands, are
better than the official lie, the deadly one. Since Hiroshima
this attitude needs little apology. Some of our best people
prefer alchemy to physics today.

There aren't many people like Miller in all literature.
The only ones I can think of are Petronius, Casanova, and
Restif. They all tried to be absolutely honest. Their books
give an overwhelming feeling of being true, the real thing,
completely uncooked. They are all intensely masculine
writers. They are all great comic writers. They all convey,
in every case very powerfully, a constant sense of the utter
tragedy of life. I can think of no more chilling, scalp-raising
passages in literature than the tolling of the bell from the
very beginning of Casanova's *Memoirs:* the comments and
asides of the aged man writing of his splendid youth, an old,
sick, friendless pauper, in a drafty castle in the backwoods
of Bohemia. And last, and most important, they were all
what the English call "spivs." Courtier of Nero or Parisian
typesetter, they were absolutely uninvolved; they just didn't
give a damn whether school kept or not.

The French like to compare Miller with Sade. But nowa-
days they like to compare everybody with Sade. It is the
currently fashionable form of Babbit-baiting over there.
The comparison is frivolous. Sade is unbelievably tedious;
Diderot stood on his head, a bigot without power, an un-
employed Robespierre. In the eighteenth century the French
writers most like Miller are the "primitive" Restif, and
Mirabeau when, in some of his personal writings, he really
works up a lather.

Miller has often been compared with Céline, but I don't
think the comparison is apposite. Céline is a man with a
thesis; furthermore, he is a littérateur. In *Journey to the
End of the Night,* he set out to write the epic of a Robinson
Crusoe of the modern soul, the utterly alienated man. He
did it, very successfully. Céline and his friends stumble
through the fog, over the muddy ruts with the body of Robinson, in a dénouement as monumental as the *Nibelungen-
lied.* But it is all a work of art. I have been in the neighbor-
hoods Céline describes. They simply aren't that awful. I am
sure on internal evidence of the story itself, that his family
wasn't that bad. And, like Malraux and some others, he is

obsessed with certain marginal sexual activities which he drags in all the time, willy-nilly.

Céline makes a sociological judgment on Robinson. Miller is Robinson, and, on the whole, he finds it a bearable role, even enjoyable in its way. The modern French writers who most resemble Miller are Carco, without the formulas, MacOrlan, if he weren't so slick, Artaud, if he weren't crazy, and Blaise Cendrars. Cendrars is a good European and Miller is only an amateur European, but Europe has been going on so long that the insights of the amateur are often much more enlightening.

Henry Miller is often spoken of as a religious writer. To some this just seems silly, because Miller is not especially profound. People expect religion to come to them vested in miracle, mystery and authority, as Dostoyevsky said. The founders of the major religions are pretty well hidden from us by the accumulation of centuries of interpretation, the dirt of history—the lie you prefer to believe. Perhaps originally they weren't so mysterious and miraculous and authoritarian. Mohammed lived in the light of history. We can form a pretty close idea of what he was like, and he wasn't very prepossessing in some ways. He was just naively direct. With the simple-mindedness of a camel driver he cut through the welter of metaphysics and mystification in the Near East of his time. Blake dressed his message up in sonorous and mysterious language; but the message itself is simple enough. D. H. Lawrence likewise. You could write it all on a postage stamp: "Mene, mene, tekel, upharsin. Your official reality is a lie. We must love one another or die." I suppose any writer who transcends conventional literature is religious in so far as he does transcend it. That is why you can never actually base an educational system on the "Hundred Best Books." A hundred of the truest insights into life as it is would destroy any educational system and its society along with it.

Certainly Miller is almost completely untouched by what is called religion in England and America and northern Europe. He is completely pagan. This is why his book on Greece, *The Colossus of Maroussi,* is a book of self-discovery as well as a very true interpretation of Greece. It is thoroughly classic. Although he never mentions Homer and dismisses the Parthenon, he did discover the life of Greece:

the common, real life of peasants and fishermen, going on, just as it has gone on ever since the Doric invasions. A world of uncompromised people, of people if not like Miller himself, at least like the man he knew he wanted to be.

His absolute freedom from the Christian or Jewish anguish of conscience, the sense of guilt, implication and compromise, makes Miller humane, maybe even humanistic, but it effectively keeps him from being humanitarian. He might cry over a pet dog who had been run over, or even punch the guilty driver in the nose. He might have assassinated Hitler if he had had the chance. He would never join the Society for the Prevention of Cruelty to Animals or the Friends' Service Committee. He is not involved in the guilt, and so in no way is he involved in the penance. This comes out in everything he writes, and it offends lots of people. Others may go to bull fights and write novels preaching the brotherhood of man. Miller just doesn't go to the bull fight in the first place. So, although he often raves, he never preaches. People have been taught to expect preaching, practically unadulterated, in even the slick fiction of the women's magazines, and they are offended now if they don't find it.

Fifty per cent of the people in this country don't vote. They simply don't want to be implicated in organized society. With, in most cases, a kind of animal instinct, they know that they cannot really do anything about it, that the participation offered them is a hoax. And even if it weren't, they know that if they don't participate, they aren't implicated, at least not voluntarily. It is for these people, the submerged fifty per cent, that Miller speaks. As the newspapers never tire of pointing out, this is a very American attitude. Millers says, "I am a patriot—of the Fourteenth Ward of Brooklyn, where I was raised." For him life has never lost that simplicity and immediacy. Politics is the deal in the saloon back room. Law is the cop on the beat, shaking down whores and helping himself to apples. Religion is Father Maguire and Rabbi Goldstein, and their actual congregations. Civilization is the Telegraph Company in *Tropic of Capricorn*. All this is a quite different story to the art critics and the literary critics and those strange people the newspapers call "pundits" and "solons."

I am sure the editors of our butcher paper liberal maga-

zines have never sat in the back room of a sawdust saloon
and listened to the politicians divide up the take from the
brothels that line the boundary streets of their wards. If
they did, they would be outraged and want to bring pressure
to bear in the State Capitol. With Miller, that is just the way
things are, and what of it?

So there isn't any social message in Miller, except an absolute one. When you get through reading the realistic novels
of James Farrell or Nelson Algren, you have a nasty suspicion that the message of the author is: "More playgrounds
and properly guided social activities will reduce crime and
vice." There is nothing especially frightful about Miller's
Brooklyn; like Farrell's South Side, it is just life in the lower
middle class and upper working class section of a big American city. It certainly isn't what queasy reviewers call it,
"the slums." It's just the life the reviewers themselves led
before they became reviewers. What outrages them is that
Miller accepts it, just as do the people who still live there.
Accepting it, how he can write about it? He can bring back
the whole pre-World War I America—the bunny hug, tunes
from *The Pink Lady,* Battling Nelson, Dempsey the Non-
pareil, Pop Anson and Pearl White, a little boy rushing the
growler with a bucket of suds and a sack of six-inch pretzels
in the smoky twilight of a Brooklyn Sunday evening.

I think that is what Miller found in Paris. Not the city of
Art, Letters and Fashion—but prewar Brooklyn. It is certainly what I like best about Paris, and it is what I get out
of Miller's writing about Paris. He is best about Paris where
it is still most like 1910 Brooklyn. He doesn't write about
the Latin Quarter, but about the dim-lit streets and dusty
little squares which lie between the Latin Quarter and the
Jardin des Plantes, where men sit drinking beer in their
shirt sleeves in front of dirty little bars in another smoky
Sunday twilight. He is better about the jumble of streets between Montrouge and Montparnasse with its polyglot and
polychrome population of the very poor, than he is about
Montparnasse itself and its artists' life. He practically ig-
nores Montmartre; apparently he concludes that only suck-
ers go there. But he writes very convincingly about that
most Brooklyn-like of all the quarters of Paris, the district
near the Military Academy on the Place du Champs de
Mars, across the river from the Eiffel Tower, where the

subway becomes an elevated, tall tenements mingle with small bankrupt factories and people sit on the doorsteps fanning themselves in the Brooklyn-like summer heat, and sleep and couple on the summer roofs.

So his intellectuals in Paris are assimilated to Brooklyn. They may talk about Neitzsche and Dostoyevsky, but they talk like hall room boys, rooming together, working at odd jobs, picking up girls in dance halls and parks. "Batching" is the word. Over the most impassioned arguments and the bawdiest conversations lingers an odor of unwashed socks. The light is the light of Welsbach mantles on detachable cuffs and unmade beds. Of course that is the way they really talked, still do for that matter.

There is a rank, old-fashioned masculinity about this world which shocks the tender-minded and self-deluded. It is far removed from the Momism of the contemporary young American male. This is why Miller is accused of writing about all women as though they were whores, never treating them as "real persons," as equals. This is why he is said to lack any sense of familial love. On the whole, I think this is true. Most of the sexual encounters in the *Tropics* and *The Rosy Crucifixion* are comic accidents, as impersonal as a pratfall. The woman never emerges at all. He characteristically writes of his wives as bad boys talk of their school teachers. When he takes his sexual relations seriously, the woman disappears in a sort of marshy cyclone. She becomes an erotic giantess, a perambulating orgy. Although Miller writes a lot about his kinship with D. H. Lawrence, he has very little of Lawrence's abiding sense of the erotic couple, of man and woman as the two equal parts of a polarity which takes up all of life. This again is Brooklyn, presuffragette Brooklyn. And I must admit that it is true, at least for almost everybody. A real wedding of equals, a truly sacramental marriage in which every bit of both personalities, and all the world with them, is transmuted and glorified may exist; in fact, some people may have a sort of talent for it, but it certainly isn't very common. And the Great Lie, the social hoax in which we live, has taken the vision of this transcendent state and turned it into its cheapest hoax and its most powerful lie. I don't see why Miller should be blamed if he has never found it. Hardly anybody ever does, and those who do usually lose it in some sordid fashion. This, of course, is the point, the message, if you want a message, of all his encounters in parks and telephone booths and brothels. Better this than the lie. Better the flesh than the World and the Devil. And this is why these passages are not pornographic, but comic like *King Lear* and tragic like *Don Quixote*.

At least once, Miller makes up for this lack. The tale of the *Cosmodemonic Telegraph Company* in *Tropic of Capricorn* is a perfect portrait of our insane and evil society. It says the same thing others have said, writing on primitive accumulation or on the condition of the working class, and it says it far more convincingly. This is human self-alienation at its uttermost, and not just theoretically, or even realistically. It is an orgy of human self alienation, a cesspool of it, and Miller rubs your nose in it. Unless you are a prig and a rascal, when you get through, you know, once and for all, what is the matter. And through it all, like Beatrice, if Beatrice had guided Dante through the Inferno, moves the figure of Valeska, who had Negro blood and who kills herself at the end—one of the most real women in fiction, if you want to call it fiction.

Once Miller used to have pinned on his bedroom door a scrap of paper. Written on it was "S'agapo"—the Greek for "I love you." In *The Alcoholic Veteran* he says, "The human heart cannot be broken."

—Kenneth Rexroth

The Alcoholic Veteran
with the Washboard Cranium

IN TULSA not long ago I saw a shorty short movie called "The Happiest Man on Earth." It was in the O. Henry style but the implications were devastating. How a picture like that could be shown in the heart of the oil fields is beyond my comprehension. At any rate it reminded me of an actual human figure whom I encountered some weeks previously in New Orleans. He too was trying to pretend that he was the happiest mortal alive.

It was about midnight and my friend Rattner and I were returning to our hotel after a jaunt through the French Quarter. As we were passing the St. Charles Hotel a man without a hat or overcoat fell into step with us and began talking about the eyeglasses he had just lost at the bar.

"It's hell to be without your glasses," he said, "especially when you're just getting over a jag. I envy you fellows. Some fool drunk in there just knocked mine off and stepped on them. Just sent a telegram to my oculist in Denver—suppose I'll have to wait a few days before they arrive. I'm just getting over one hell of a binge: it must have lasted a week or more. I don't know what day it is or what's happened in the world since I fell off the wagon. I just stepped out to get a breath of air—and some food. I never eat when I'm on a bat—the alcohol keeps me going. There's nothing to do about it, of course; I'm a confirmed alcoholic. Incurable. I know all about the subject—studied medicine before I took up law. I've tried all the cures, read all the theories. . . . Why look here—" and he reached into his breast pocket and extricated a mass of papers along with a thick wallet which fell to the ground—"look at this, here's an article on the subject I wrote myself. Funny, what? It was just published recently in . . ." (he mentioned a well-known publication with a huge circulation).

17

I stooped down to pick up the wallet and the calling cards which had fluttered out and fallen into the gutter. He was holding the loose bundle of letters and documents in one hand and gesticulating eloquently with the other. He seemed to be utterly unconcerned about losing any of his papers or even about the contents of the wallet. He was raving about the ignorance and stupidity of the medical profession. They were a bunch of quacks; they were hijackers; they were criminal-minded. And so on.

It was cold and rainy and we, who were bundled up in overcoats, were urging him to get moving.

"Oh, don't worry about that," he said, with a good-natured grin, "I never catch cold. I must have left my hat and coat in the bar. The air feels good," and he threw his coat open wide as if to let the mean, penetrating night wind percolate through the thin covering in which he was wrapped. He ran his fingers through his shock of curly blond hair and wiped the corners of his mouth with a soiled handkerchief. He was a man of good stature with a rather weather-beaten face, a man who evidently lived an outdoor life. The most distinctive thing about him was his smile—the warmest, frankest, most ingratiating smile I've ever seen on a man's face. His gestures were jerky and trembly, which was only natural considering the state of his nerves. He was all fire and energy, like a man who has just had a shot in the arm. He talked well, too, exceedingly well, as though he might have been a journalist as well as doctor and lawyer. And he was very obviously not trying to make a touch.

When we had walked a block or so he stopped in front of a cheap eating house and invited us to step in with him and have something to eat or drink. We told him we were on our way home, that we were tired and eager to get to bed.

"But only for a few minutes," he said. "I'm just going to have a quick bite."

Again we tried to beg off. But he persisted, taking us by the arm and leading us to the door of the café. I repeated that I was going home but suggested to Rattner that he might stay if he liked. I started to disengage myself from his grasp.

"Look," he said, suddenly putting on a grave air, "you've got to do me this little favor. I've got to talk to you people. I might do something desperate if you don't. I'm asking you as a human kindness—you wouldn't refuse to give a man a little time, would you, when you knew that it meant so much to him?"

With that of course we surrendered without a word. "We're in for it now," I thought to myself, feeling a little disgusted with myself for letting myself be tricked by a sentimental drunkard.

"What are you going to have?" he said, ordering himself a plate of ham and beans which, before he had even brought it to the table, he sprinkled liberally with ketchup and chili sauce. As he was about to remove it from the counter he turned to the server and ordered him to get another plate of ham and beans ready. "I can eat three or four of these in a row," he explained, "when I begin to sober up." We had ordered coffee for ourselves. Rattner was about to take the checks when our friend reached for them and stuck them in his pocket. "This is on me," he said, "I invited you in here."

We tried to protest but he silenced us by saying, between huge gulps which he washed down with black coffee, that money was one of the things that never bothered him.

"I don't know how much I've got on me now," he continued. "Enough for this anyway. I gave my car to a dealer yesterday to sell for me. I drove down here from Idaho with some old cronies from the bench—they were on a jamboree. I used to be in the legislature once," and he mentioned some Western State where he had served. "I can ride back free on the railroad," he added. "I have a pass. I used to be somebody once upon a time. . . ." He interrupted himself to go to the counter and get another helping.

As he sat down again, while dousing the beans with ketchup and chili sauce, he reached with his left hand into his breast pocket and dumped the whole contents of his pocket on the table. "You're an artist aren't you?" he said to Rattner. "And you're a writer, I can tell that," he said, looking at me. "You don't have to tell me, I sized you both up immediately." He was pushing the papers about as he spoke, still energetically shoveling down his food, and apparently poking about for some articles which he had written and which he wanted to show us. "I write a bit myself," he said, "whenever I need a little extra change. You see, as soon as I get my allowance I go on a bat. Well, when I come out of it I sit down and write some crap for"—and here he mentioned some of the leading magazines, those with the big circulation. "I can always make a few hundred dollars that way, if I want to. There's nothing to it. I don't say it's literature, of course. But who wants literature? Now where in the hell is that story I wrote about a psychopathic case . . . I just wanted to show you that I know what I'm talking about. You see. . . ." He broke off suddenly and gave us a rather wry, twisted smile, as though it were hopeless to try to put it all in words. He had a forkful of beans which he was about to shovel down. He dropped the fork, like an automaton, the beans spilling all over his soiled letters and documents, and leaning over the table he startled me by seizing my arm and placing my hand on his skull, rubbing it roughly back and forth. "Feel that?" he said, with a queer gleam in his eye. "Just like a washboard, eh?" I pulled my hand away as quickly as I could. The feel of that corrugated brainpan gave me the creeps. "That's just one item," he said. And with that he rolled up his sleeve and showed us a jagged wound that ran from the wrist to the elbow. Then he pulled up the leg of his trousers. More horrible wounds. As if that were not enough he stood up quickly, pulled off his coat and, quite as if there were no one but just us three in the place, he opened his shirt and displayed even uglier scars. As he was putting on his coat he looked boldly around and in clear, ringing tones he sang with terrible bitter mockery "America, I love you!" Just the opening phrase. Then he sat down as abruptly as he had gotten up and quietly proceeded to finish the ham and beans. I thought there would be a commotion but no, people continued eating and talking just as before, only now we had become the center of attention. The man at the cash register seemed rather nervous and thoroughly undecided as to what to do. I wondered what next.

I half expected our friend to raise his voice and begin a melodramatic scene. Except however for the fact that he had grown a little more high-strung and more voluble his behavior was not markedly different from before. But his tone had altered. He spoke now in jerky phrases punctuated with the most blasphemous oaths and accompanied by grimaces which were frightening to behold. The demon in him seemed to be coming out. Or rather, the mutilated being who had been wounded and humiliated beyond all human endurance.

"Mister Roosevelt!" he said, his voice full of scorn and contempt. "I was just listening to him over the radio. Getting us in shape to fight England's battles again, what? Conscription. *Not this bird!"* and he jerked his thumb backwards viciously. "Decorated three times on the field of battle. The Argonne . . . Château Thierry . . . the Somme . . . concussion of the brain . . . fourteen months in the hospital outside Paris . . . ten months on this side of the water. Making murderers of us and then begging us to settle down quietly and go to work again. . . . Wait a minute, I want to read you a poem I wrote about our Fuehrer the other night." He fished among the papers lying about on the table. He got up to get himself another cup of coffee and as he stood with cup in hand, sipping it, he began to read aloud this vituperative, scabrous poem about the President. Surely now, I thought, somebody will take umbrage and start a fight. I looked at Rattner who believes in Roosevelt, who had traveled 1200 miles to vote for him at the last election. Rattner was silent. He probably thought it useless to remonstrate with a man who had obviously been shell shocked. Still, I couldn't help thinking, the situation was a little unusual, to say the least. A phrase I had heard in Georgia came back to my head. It was from the lips of a woman who had just been to see "Lincoln in Illinois." "What are they trying to do—make a *he*-ro of that man Lincoln?" Yes, something distinctly pre-Civil War about the atmosphere. A president re-elected to office by a great popular vote and yet his name was anathema to millions. Another Woodrow Wilson per-

chance? Our friend wouldn't even accord him that rank-
ing. He had sat down again and in a fairly moderate tone
of voice he began making sport of the politicians, the
members of the judiciary, the generals and admirals, the
quartermaster generals, the Red Cross, the Salvation
Army, the Y. M. C. A. A withering play of mockery and
cynicism, larded with personal experiences, grotesque encounters, buffoonish pranks which only a battle-scarred
veteran would have the audacity to relate.

"And so," he exploded, "they wanted to parade me like
a monkey, with my uniform and medals. They had the
brass band out and the mayor all set to give us a glorious
welcome. The town is yours, boys, and all that hokum.
Our heroes! God, it makes me vomit to think of it. I
ripped the medals off my uniform and threw them away.
I burned the damned uniform in the fireplace. Then I got
myself a quart of rye and I locked myself in my room. I
drank and wept, all by myself. Outside the band was playing and people cheering hysterically. I was all black inside.
Everything I had believed in was gone. All my illusions
were shattered. They broke my heart, that's what they did.
They didn't leave me a god-damned crumb of solace. Except the booze, of course. Sure, they tried to take that
away from me too, at first. They tried to shame me into
giving it up. *Shame me,* huh! Me who had killed hundreds
of men with the bayonet, who lived like an animal and lost
all sense of human decency. They can't do anything to
shame *me,* or frighten me, or fool me, or bribe me, or
trick me. I know them inside out, the dirty bastards.
They've starved me and beaten me and put me behind the
bars. That stuff doesn't frighten me. I can put up with
hunger, cold, thirst, lice, vermin, disease, blows, insults,
degradation, fraud, theft, libel, slander, betrayal . . . I've
been through the whole works . . . they've tried everything
on me . . . and still they can't crush me, can't stop my
mouth, can't make me say it's right. I don't want anything to do with these honest, God-fearing people. They
sicken me. I'd rather live with animals—or cannibals."
He found a piece of sheet music among his papers and
documents. "There's a song I wrote three years ago. It's
sentimental but it won't do anyone any harm. I can only

write music when I'm drunk. The alcohol blots out the pain. I've still got a heart, a big one, too. My world is a world of memories. Do you remember this one?" He began to hum a familiar melody. "You wrote that?" I said, taken by surprise. "Yes, I wrote that—and I wrote others too"—and he began to reel off the titles of his songs.

I was just beginning to wonder about the truth of all these statements—lawyer, doctor, legislator, scrivener, song writer—when he began to talk about his inventions. He had made three fortunes, it seems, before he fell into complete disgrace. It was getting pretty thick even for me, and I'm a credulous individual, when presently a chance remark he made about a friend of his, a famous architect in the Middle West, drew a surprising response from Rattner. "He was my buddy in the army," said Rattner quietly. "Well," said our friend, "he married my sister." With this there began a lively exchange of reminiscences between the two of them, leaving not the slightest doubt in my mind that our friend was telling the truth, at least so far as the architect was concerned.

From the architect to the construction of a great house in the center of Texas somewhere was but a step. With the last fortune he made he had bought himself a ranch, married and built himself a fantastic chateau in the middle of nowhere. The drinking was gradually tailing off. He was deeply in love with his wife and looking forward to raising a family. Well, to make a long story short, a friend of his persuaded him to go to Alaska with him on a mining speculation. He left his wife behind because he feared the climate would be too rigorous for her. He was away about a year. When he returned—he had come back without warning, thinking to surprise her—he found her in bed with his best friend. With a whip he drove the two of them out of the house in the dead of night, in a blinding snowstorm, not even giving them a chance to put their clothes on. Then he got the bottle out, of course, and after he had had a few shots he began to smash things up. But the house was so damned big that he soon grew tired of that sport. There was only one way to make a good job of it and that was to put a match to the works, which he did. Then he got in his car and drove off, not bothering to even pack a valise. A few days later, in a distant State, he picked up the newspaper and learned that his friend had been found dead of exposure. Nothing was said about the wife. In fact, he never learned what happened to her from that day since. Shortly after this incident he got in a brawl with a man at a bar and cracked his skull open with a broken bottle. That meant a stretch at hard labor for eighteen months, during which time he made a study of prison conditions and proposed certain reforms to the Governor of the State which were accepted and put into practice.

"I was very popular," he said. "I have a good voice and I can entertain a bit. I kept them in good spirits while I was there. Later I did another stretch. It doesn't bother me at all. I can adjust myself to most any conditions. Usually there's a piano and a billiard table and books—and if you can't get anything to drink you can always get yourself a little dope. I switch back and forth. What's the difference? All a man wants is to forget the present. . . ."

"Yes, but can you really forget?" Rattner interjected.

"*I* can! You just give me a piano, a quart of rye and a sociable little joint and I can be just as happy as a man wants to be. You see, I don't need all the paraphernalia you fellows require. All I carry with me is a toothbrush. If I want a shave I buy one; if I want to change my linen I get new linen; when I'm hungry I eat; when I'm tired I sleep. It doesn't make much difference to me whether I sleep in a bed or on the ground. If I want to write a story I go to a newspaper office and borrow a machine. If I want to go to Boston all I have to do is show my pass. Any place is home sweet home so long as I can find a place to drink and meet a friendly fellow like myself. I don't pay taxes and I don't pay rent. I have no boss, no responsibilities. I don't vote and I don't care who's President or Vice-President. I don't want to make money and I don't look for fame or success. What can you offer me that I haven't got, eh? I'm a free man—*are you?* And happy. I'm happy because I don't care what happens. All I want is my quart of whiskey every day—a bottle of forgetfulness, that's all. My health? I never worry about it. I'm just as strong and healthy as the next man. If there's anything wrong with me I don't know it. I might live to be a hundred whereas you guys are probably worrying whether you'll live to be sixty. There's only one day— *today*. If I feel good I write a poem and throw it away the next day. I'm not trying to win any literary prizes—I'm just expressing myself in my own cantankerous way. . . ."

At this point he began to go off the track about his literary ability. His vanity was getting the best of him. When it got to the point where he insisted that I glance at a story he had written for some popular magazine I thought it best to pull him up short. I much preferred to hear about the desperado and the drunkard than the man of letters.

"Look here," I said, not mincing my words, "you admit that this is all crap, don't you? Well, I never read crap. What's the use of showing me that stuff—I don't doubt that you can write as badly as the next fellow—it doesn't take genius to do that. What I'm interested in is good writing: I admire genius not success. Now if you have anything that you're proud of that's another thing. I'd be glad to read something that you yourself thought well of."

He gave me a long, down-slanting look. For a few long moments he looked at me that way, silently, scrutinizingly. "I'll tell you," he said finally, "there's just one thing I've ever written which I think good—and I've never put it down on paper. But I've got it up here," and he tapped his forehead with his forefinger. "If you'd like to hear it I'll recite it for you. It's a long poem I wrote one time when I was in Manila. You've heard of Morro Castle, haven't you? All right, it was just outside the walls of Morro Castle that I got the inspiration. I think it's a great poem. I *know* it is! I wouldn't want to see it printed. I wouldn't want to take money for it. Here it is. . . ."

Without pausing to clear his throat or take a drink he launched into this poem about the sun going down in Manila. He recited it at a rapid pace in a clear musical voice. It was like shooting down the rapids in a light canoe. All around us the conversation had died down; some stood up and moved in close the better to hear him. It seemed to have neither beginning nor end. As I say, it had started off at the velocity of a flood, and it went on and on, image upon image, crescendo upon crescendo, rising and falling in musical cadences. I don't remember a single line of it, more's the pity. All I remember is the sensation I had of being borne along on the swollen bosom of a great river through the heart of a tropical zone in which there was a constant fluttering of dazzling plumage, the sheen of wet green leaves, the bending and swaying of lakes of grass, the throbbing midnight blue of sky, the gleam of stars like coruscating jewels, the song of birds intoxicated by God knows what. There was a fever running through the lines, the fever not of a sick man but of an exalted, frenzied creature who had suddenly found his true voice and was trying it out in the dark. It was a voice which issued straight from the heart, a taut, vibrant column of blood which fell upon the ear in rhapsodic, thunderous waves. The end was an abatement rather than a cessation, a diminuendo which brought the pounding rhythm to a whisper that prolonged itself far beyond the actual silence in which it finally merged. The voice had ceased to register, but the poem continued to pulsate in the echoing cells of the brain.

He broke the silence which ensued by alluding modestly to his unusual facility for memorizing whatever caught his eye. "I remember everything I read in school," he said, "from Longfellow and Wordsworth to Ronsard and François Villon. *Villon,* there's a fellow after my own heart," and he launched into a familiar verse in an accent that betrayed he had more than a textbook knowledge of French. "The greatest poets were the Chinese," he said. "They made the little things reveal the greatness of the universe. They were philosophers first and then poets. They *lived* their poetry. We have nothing to make poetry about, except death and desolation. You can't make a poem about an automobile or a telephone booth. To begin with, the heart has to be intact. One must be able to believe in something. The values we were taught to respect when we were children are all smashed. We're not men any more—we're automatons. We don't even get any satisfaction in killing. The last war killed off our impulses. We don't respond; we react. We're the lost legion of the defeated archangels. We're dangling in chaos and our lead-ers, blinder than bats, bray like jackasses. You wouldn't call Mister Roosevelt a great leader, would you? Not if you know your history. A leader has to be inspired by a great vision; he has to lift his people out of the mire with mighty pinions; he has to rouse them from the stupor in which they vegetate like stoats and slugs. You don't advance the cause of freedom and humanity by leading poor, feeble dreamers to the slaughterhouse. What's he bellyaching about anyway? Did the Creator appoint him the Saviour of Civilization? When I went over there to fight for Democracy I was just a kid. I didn't have any great ambitions, neither did I have any desire to kill anybody. I was brought up to believe that the shedding of blood was a crime against God and man. Well, I did what they asked me to, like a good soldier. I murdered every son of a bitch that was trying to murder me. What else could I do? It wasn't all murder, of course. I had some good times now and then—a different sort of pleasure than I ever figured I would like. In fact, nothing was like what I thought it would be before I went over. You know what those bastards make you into. Why, your own mother wouldn't recognize you if she saw you taking your pleasure—or crawling in the mud and sticking a bayonet in a man who never did you any harm. I'm telling you, it got so filthy and poisonous I didn't know who I was any more. I was just a number that lit up like a switchboard when the order came to do this, do that, do the other thing. You couldn't call me a man—I didn't have a god-damned bit of feeling left. And I wasn't an animal because if I had been an animal I'd have had better sense than to get myself into such a mess. Animals kill one another only when they're hungry. We kill because we're afraid of our own shadow, afraid that if we used a little common sense we'd have to admit that our glorious principles were wrong. Today I haven't got any principles—I'm an outlaw. I have only one ambition left—to get enough booze under my belt every day so as to forget what the world looks like. I never sanctioned this setup. You can't convince me that I murdered all those Germans in order to bring this unholy mess about. No sir, I refuse to take any part in it. I wash my hands of it. I walk out on it. Now if that makes me a bad citizen why then I'm a bad citizen. So what? Do you suppose if I ran around like a mad dog, begging for a club and a rifle to start murdering all over again, do you suppose that would make me into a good citizen, good enough, what I mean, to vote the straight Democratic ticket? I suppose if I did that I could eat right out of their hand, what? Well, I don't want to eat out of anybody's hand. I want to be left alone; I want to dream my dreams, to believe as I once believed, that life is good and beautiful and that men can live with one another in peace and plenty. No son of a bitch on earth can tell me that to make life better you have to first kill a million or ten million men in cold blood. No sir, those bastards haven't got any heart. I know the Germans are no worse than we are, and by Christ, I know from experience that some of them at least are a damned sight better than the French or the English.

"That schoolteacher we made a President of, he thought he had everything fixed just right, didn't he? Can you picture him crawling around on the floor at Versailles like an old billygoat, putting up imaginary fences with a blue pencil? What's the sense of making new boundaries, will you tell me? Why tariffs and taxes and sentry boxes and pillboxes anyway? Why doesn't England part with some of her unlawful possessions? If the poor people in England can't make a living when the government possesses the biggest empire that ever was how are they going to make a living when the empire falls to pieces? Why don't they emigrate to Canada or Africa or Australia?

"There's another thing I don't understand. We always assume that we're in the right, that we have the best government under the sun. How do we know—have we tried the others out? Is everything running so beautifully here that we couldn't bear the thought of a change? Supposing I honestly believed in Fascism or Communism or polygamy or Mohammedanism or pacifism or any of the things that are now tabu in this country? What would happen to me if I started to open my trap, eh? Why you don't even dare to protest against being vaccinated, though there's plenty of evidence to prove that vaccination does more harm than good. Where is this liberty and freedom we boast about?

You're only free if you're in good odor with your neighbors, and even then it's not a hell of a lot of rope they give you. If you happen to be broke and out of a job your freedom isn't worth a button. And if you're old besides then it's just plain misery. They're much kinder to animals and flowers and crazy people. Civilization is a blessing to the unfit and the degenerate—the others it breaks or demoralizes. As far as the comforts of life go I'm better off when I'm in jail than when I'm out. In the one case they take your freedom away and in the other they take your manhood. If you play the game you can have automobiles and town houses and mistresses and *pâté de foie gras* and all the folderol that goes with it. But who wants to play the game? Is it worth it? Did you ever see a millionaire who was happy or who had any self-respect? Did you ever go to Washington and see our lawbreakers—excuse me, I mean lawmakers—in session? There's a sight for you! If you dressed them in striped dungarees and put them behind the bars with pick and shovel nobody on earth could tell but what they belonged there. Or take that rogues' gallery of Vice-Presidents. I was standing in front of a drug store not so long ago studying their physiognomies. There never was a meaner, craftier, uglier, more fanatical bunch of human faces ever assembled in one group. And that's the stuff they make presidents of whenever there's an assassination. Yes, assassinations. I was sitting in a restaurant the day after the election—up in Maine it was —and the fellow next to me was trying to lay a bet with another guy that Roosevelt wouldn't last the term out. He was laying five to one—but nobody would take him up. The thing that struck me was that the waitress, whom nobody had paid any attention to, suddenly remarked in a quiet tone that 'we were about due for another assassination.' Assassinations seem ugly when it's the President of the United States but there's plenty of assassinating going on all the time and nobody seems to get very riled up about it. Where I was raised we used to flog a nigger to death just to show a visitor how it's done. It's still being done, but not so publicly, I suppose. We improve things by covering them up.

"You take the food they hand us. . . . Of course I

haven't got any taste left, from all the booze I pour down my system. But a man who has any taste buds left must be in a hell of a way eating the slop they hand you in public places. Now they're discovering that the vitamins are missing. So what do they do? Do they change the diet, change the chef? No, they give you the same rotten slop only they add the necessary vitamins. That's civilization—always doing things assways. Well, I'll tell you, I'm so god-damned civilized now that I prefer to take my poison straight. If I had lived what they call a 'normal' life I'd be on the dump heap by fifty anyway. I'm forty-eight now and sound as a whistle, always doing just the opposite of what they recommend. If you were to live the way I do for two weeks you'd be in the hospital. So what does it add up to, will you tell me? If I didn't drink I'd have some other vice— a baby-snatcher, maybe, or a refined Jack-the-Ripper, who knows? And if I didn't have any vices I'd be just a poor sap, a sucker like millions of others, and where would that get me? Do you think I'd get any satisfaction out of dying in harness, as they say? Not me! I'd rather die in the alcoholic ward among the has-beens and no-goods. At least, if it happens that way, I'll have the satisfaction of saying that I had only one master—John Barleycorn. You have a thousand masters, perfidious, insidious ones who torment you even in your sleep. I've only got one, and to tell the truth he's more like a friend than a taskmaster. He gets me into some nasty messes, but he never lies to me. He never says 'freedom, liberty, equality' or any of that rot. He just says, 'I will make you so stinking drunk that you won't know who you are,' and that's all I crave. Now if Mister Roosevelt or any other politician could make me a promise and keep it I'd have a little respect for him. But who ever heard of a diplomat or a politician keeping his word? It's like expecting a millionaire to give his fortune away to the men and women he robbed it from. It just ain't done."

He went on at this rate without a letup—long monologues about the perfidy, the cruelty and the injustice of man towards man. Really a grand fellow at heart, with good instincts and all the attributes of a citizen of the world, except for the fact that somewhere along the line he had been flung out of the societal orbit and could never get back into it again. I saw from the queries which Rattner interjected now and then that he had hopes for the man. At two in the morning he was optimistic enough to believe that with a little perseverance there might be sown in this rugged heart the seed of hope. To me, much as I liked the fellow, it seemed just as futile as to attempt to reclaim the bad lands of Arizona or Dakota. The only thing society can do with such people, and it never does, is to be kind and indulgent to them. Just as the earth itself, in its endless experiments, comes to a dead end in certain regions, gives up, as it were, so with individuals. The desire to kill the soul, for that's what it amounts to, is a phenomenon which has an extraordinary fascination for me. Sometimes it lends a grandeur to an individual which seems to rival the sublime struggles of those men whom we consider superior types. Because the gesture of negation, when pure and uncompromising, has also in it the qualities of the heroic. Weaklings are incapable of flinging themselves away in this manner. The weakling merely succumbs while the other, more single-minded character works hand and glove with Fate, egging it on, as it were, and mocking it at the same time. To invoke Fate is to expose oneself to the chaos which the blind forces of the universe are ever ready to set in motion once the will of man is broken. The man of destiny is the extreme opposite: in him we have an example of the miraculous nature of man, in that those same blind forces appear to be harnessed and controlled, directed towards the fulfillment of man's own microscopic purpose. But to act either way one has to lift himself completely out of the set, reactionary pattern of the ordinary individual. Even to vote for self-destruction demands something of a cosmic approach. A man has to have some definite view of the nature of the world in order to reject it. It is far easier to commit suicide than to kill the soul. There remains the doubt, which not even the most determined destroyer can annihilate, that the task is impossible. If it could be accomplished by an act of will then there would be no need to summon Fate. But it is precisely because the will no longer functions that the hopeless individual surrenders to the powers that be. In short he is obliged to renounce the one act which would deliver him of his torment. Our friend had delivered himself up to John Barleycorn. But beyond a certain point John Barleycorn is powerless to operate. Could one succeed in summoning all the paralyzing and inhibiting forces of the universe there would still remain a frontier, a barrier which nothing but man himself can surmount and invade. The body can be killed, but the soul is imperishable. A man like our friend could have killed himself a thousand times had he the least hope of solving his problem thereby. But he had chosen to relapse, to lie cold and inert like the moon, to crush every fructifying impulse and, by imitating death, finally achieve it in the very heart of his being.

When he spoke it was the heart which cried out. They had broken his heart, he said, but it was not true. The heart cannot be broken. The heart can be wounded and cause the whole universe to appear as one vast writhing place of anguish. But the heart knows no limits in its ability to endure suffering and torment. Were it otherwise the race would have perished long ago. As long as the heart pumps blood it pumps life. And life can be lived at levels so utterly disparate one from another that in some cases it would appear to be almost extinct. There are just as violent contrasts in the way life is lived by human beings as there are startling contrasts in the fish, the mineral or the vegetable worlds. When we use the term human society we speak of something which defies definition. No one can encompass the thought and behavior of man with a word or phrase. Human beings move in constellations which, unlike the stars, are anything but fixed. A story, such as I am relating, can be of interest or significance to certain clusters of men and totally devoid of any charm or value to others. What would Shakespeare mean to a Patagonian, assuming he could be taught to read the words? What can "The Varieties of Religious Experience" mean to a Hopi Indian? A man goes along thinking the world to be thus and so, simply because he has never been jolted out of the rut in which he crawls like a worm. For the civilized man war is not always the greatest jolt to his smug every day pattern. Some men, and their number is greater I fear than most us would like to believe, find war an exciting if not altogether agreeable interruption to the toil and drudgery

of common life. The presence of death adds spice, quickens
their usually torpid brain cells. But there are others, like
our friend who, in their revolt against wanton killing, in
the bitter realization that no power of theirs will ever put
an end to it, elect to withdraw from society and if possible
destroy even the chance of returning to earth again at
some distant and more propitious moment in human history. They want nothing more to do with man; they want
to nip the experiment in the bud. And of course they are
just as powerless here as in their efforts to eliminate war.
But they are a fascinating species of man and ultimately of
value to the race, if for no other reason than that they act
as semaphores in those periods of darkness when we seem
to be rushing headlong to destruction. The one who op-
erates the switchboard remains invisible and it is in him we
put our trust, but as long as we hug the rails the flashing
semaphores offer a fleeting consolation. We hope that the
engineer will bring us safely to our destination. We sit with
arms folded and surrender our safekeeping to other hands.
But even the best engineer can only take us over a charted
course. Our adventure is in uncharted realms, with cour-
age, intelligence and faith as our only guides. If we have a
duty it is to put our trust in our own powers. No man is
great enough or wise enough for any of us to surrender our
destiny to. The only way in which any one can lead us is
to restore to us the belief in our own guidance. The greatest men have always reaffirmed this thought. But the men
who dazzle us and lead us astray are the men who promise
us those things which no man can honestly promise another—namely safety, security, peace, etc. And the most
deceptive of all such promisers are those who bid us kill
one another in order to attain the fictive goal.

Like our friend, thousands, perhaps millions of men,
awaken to the realization of their error on the battlefield.
When it is too late. When the men whom they no longer
have a desire to kill are already upon them, ready to cut
their throats. Then it is kill or be killed and whether one
kills in the knowledge of the truth or without that knowledge makes little difference. The murdering goes on—until
the day the sirens scream their announcement of a truce.
When peace comes it descends upon a world too exhausted

to show any reaction except a dumb feeling of relief. The men at the helm, who were spared the horrors of combat, now play their ignominious role in which greed and hatred rival one another for mastery. The men who bore the brunt of the struggle are too sickened and disgusted to show any desire to participate in the rearrangement of the world. All they ask is to be left alone to enjoy the luxury of the petty, workaday rhythm which once seemed so dull and barren. How different the new order would be if we could consult the veteran instead of the politician! But logic has it that we ordain innocent millions to slaughter one another, and when the sacrifice is completed, we authorize a handful of bigoted, ambitious men who have never known what it is to suffer to rearrange our lives. What chance has a lone individual to dissent when he has nothing to sanction his protest except his wounds? Who cares about wounds when the war is over? Get them out of sight, all these wounded and maimed and mutilated! Resume work! Take up life where you left off, those of you who are still strong and able! The dead will be given monuments; the mutilated will be pensioned off. Let's get on—business as usual and no feeble sentimentality about the horrors of war. When the next war comes we'll be ready for them! *Und so weiter.* . . .

I was reflecting thus while he and Rattner were exchanging anecdotes about their experiences in France. I was dying to get to bed. Our friend, on the other hand, was obviously becoming more awake; I knew that with the least encouragement he would regale us till dawn with his stories. The more he talked about his misfortunes, oddly enough, the more cheerful he seemed to grow. By the time we managed to persuade him to leave the place he was positively radiant. Out in the street he began bragging again about his wonderful condition — liver, kidneys, bowels, lungs all perfect, eyes super-normal. He had forgotten evidently about his broken glasses, or perhaps that was just an invention by way of breaking the ice.

We had a few blocks to walk before reaching our hotel. He said he would accompany us because he was going to turn in soon himself. There were some thirty-five cent lodging houses in the vicinity, he thought, where he'd get a few hours sleep. Every few steps, it seemed, he stopped dead and planted himself in front of us to expatiate on some incident which he evidently thought it important for us to hear. Or was it an unconscious desire to delay us in nestling down to our warm cozy beds? More than once, when we finally neared the hotel, we held out our hands to say good night, only to drop them again and stand patiently with one foot in the gutter and one on the curb hearing him out to the end.

At last I began to wonder if he had the necessary pence to get himself a flop. Just as I was about to inquire Rattner, whose thoughts were evidently running in the same direction, anticipated me. Had he the money for a room? Why, he was pretty certain he did; he had counted his change at the restaurant. Yes, he was quite sure he had enough—and if he hadn't he would ask us to make it up. Anyhow, that wasn't important. What was he saying? Oh yes, about Nevada . . . about the crazy ghost towns he had lived in . . . the saloon made of beer bottles and the mechanical piano from the Klondike which he rolled out to the desert one night just to hear how it would sound in that great empty space. Yes, the only people worth talking to were the bar flies. They were all living in the past, like himself. Some day he'd write the whole thing out. "Why bother to do that?" I interposed. "Maybe you're right," he said, running his tobacco-stained fingers through his thick curly hair. "I'm going to ask you for a cigarette now," he said. "I'm all out of mine." As we lit the cigarette for him he launched into another tale. "Listen," I said, "make it short, will you, I'm dead tired." We moved at a snail-like pace across the street to the door of the hotel. As he was winding up his story I put my hand on the handle of the door in readiness to make a break. We started to shake hands again when suddenly he took it into his head to count his change. "I guess I'll have to borrow three cents from you," he said. "You can have a couple of bucks if you like," we both started to say simultaneously. No, he didn't want that—that might start him drinking all over again. He didn't want to begin that now—he wanted a little rest first.

There was nothing to do but give him the three cents

and what cigarettes we had left. It hurt Rattner to hand him three pennies. "Why don't you take a half dollar at least?" he said. "You might use it for breakfast tomorrow."

"If you give me a half dollar," he said, "I'll probably buy some candles and put them at Robert E. Lee's monument up the street. It was his birthday today, you know. People have forgotten about him already. Everybody's snoring now. I sort of like Lee; I revere his memory. He was more than a great general—he was a man of great delicacy and understanding. As a matter of fact, I think I'll wander up there anyway before turning in. It's just the sort of fool thing a fellow like me would do. Sleep isn't so important. I'll go up there to the monument and talk to him a little while. Let the world sleep! You see, I'm free to do as I please. I'm really better off than a millionaire. . . ."

"Then there's nothing more we can do for you?" I said, cutting him short. "You've got everything you need, you've got your health, you're happy. . . ."

I had no more than uttered the word happy when his face suddenly changed and, grasping me by both arms with a steely grip, he wheeled me around and gazing into my eyes with a look I shall never forget, he broke forth: *"Happy?* Listen, you're a writer—*you* should know better than that. You know I'm lying like hell. *Happy?* Why, brother, you're looking at the most miserable man on earth." He paused a moment to brush away a tear. He was still holding me firmly with both hands, determined apparently that I should hear him out. "I didn't bump into you accidentally tonight," he continued. "I saw you coming along and I sized you both up. I knew you were artists and that's why I collared you. I always pick the people I want to talk to. I didn't lose my glasses at the bar, nor did I give my car to a dealer to sell for me. But everything else I told you is true. I'm just hoofing it from place to place. I've only been out of the pen a few weeks. They've got their eye on me still—somebody's been trailing me around town. I'm giving them the runaround. If I should go up to the circle now and accidentally fall asleep on a bench they'd have the goods on me. But I'm too wary for that. I'll just amble about leisurely and when I'm good and ready I'll turn in. The bartender'll fix me up in the morning . . . Look, I don't know what kind of stuff you write, but if you'll take a tip from me the thing to do is to learn what it is to suffer. No writer is any good unless he's suffered. . . ."

At this point Rattner was about to say something in my behalf, but I motioned to him to be silent. It was a strange thing for me to be listening to a man urging me to suffer. I had always been of the opinion that I had had more than my share of suffering. Evidently it didn't show on my face. Or else the fellow was so engrossed with his own misfortunes that he was unable or unwilling to recognize the marks in another. So I let him ramble on. I listened to the last drop without once seeking to interrupt him. When he had finished I held out my hand for the last time to say good-bye. He took my hand in both of his and clasped it warmly. "I've talked your head off, haven't I?" he said, that strange ecstatic smile lighting up his face. "Look, my name is So-and-So." It sounded like Allison or Albertson. He began digging for his wallet. "I'd like to give you an address," he said, "where you could drop me a line." He was searching for something to write on, but couldn't seem to find a card or blank piece of paper among the litter of documents he carried in that thick wallet. "Well, you give me yours," he said. "That will do. I'll write you some time."

Rattner was writing out his name and address for the fellow. He took the card and put it carefully in his wallet. He waited for me to write mine.

"I have no address," I said. "Besides, we've got nothing more to say to each other. I don't think we'll ever meet again. You're bent on destroying yourself, and I can't stop you, nor can anybody else. What's the good of pretending that we'll write one another? Tomorrow I'll be somewhere else and so will you. All I can say is I wish you luck." With that I pulled the door open and walked into the lobby of the hotel. Rattner was still saying good-bye to him.

As I stood there waiting for the elevator boy he waved his hand cheerily. I waved back. Then he stood a moment, swaying on his heels and apparently undecided whether to go towards the monument or turn round and look for a flop. Just as the elevator boy started the lift going he signalled for us to wait. I signalled back that it was too late. "Go on up," I said to the boy. As we rose up out of sight our friend stood there in front of the hotel door peering up at us with a blank expression. I didn't feel that it was a lousy thing to do, leave him standing there like that. I looked at Rattner to see how he felt about it. He sort of shrugged his shoulders. "What can you do with a guy like that?" he said, "he won't let you help him." As we entered the room and turned on the lights, he added: "You surely did give him a jolt when you told him he was happy. Do you know what I thought he was going to do? I thought he was going to crack you. Did you notice the look that came over him? And when you refused to give him your name and address, well that just about finished him. I couldn't do that. I'm not reproaching you—I just wonder *why* you acted that way. You could just as well have let him down easy, couldn't you?"

I was about to smile, but so many thoughts entered my head at once that I forgot and instead I frowned.

"Don't get me wrong," said Rattner, misinterpreting my expression. "I think you were damned patient with him. You hardly said a word all evening."

"No, it's not that," I said. "I'm not thinking of myself. I'm thinking of all the fellows like him I've met in one short lifetime. Listen, did I ever tell you about my experience with the telegraph company? Hell, it's late and I know you're fagged out. So am I. But I just want to tell you one or two things. I'm not trying to defend myself, mind you. I'm guilty, if you like. Maybe I could have done something, said something—I don't know what or how. Sure, I did let him down. And what's more I probably hurt him deeply. But I figured it would do him good, if you can believe that. I never crossed him once, did I, or criticized him, or urged him to change his ways? No, I never do that. If a man is determined to go to the dogs I help him—I give him a little push if needs be. If he wants to get on his feet I help him to do that. Whatever he asks for. I believe in letting a man do as he pleases, for good or bad, because eventually we'll all wind up in the same place.

But what I was starting to tell you is this—I've heard so many terrible tales, met so many guys like this Allison or Albertson, that I've hardly got an ounce of sympathy left in me. That's a horrible thing to say, but it's true. Get this —in one day, sometimes, I've had as many as a half-dozen men break down and weep before me, beg me to do something for them, or if not for them, for their wives and children. In four years I hardly ever had more than four or five hours' sleep a night, largely because I was trying to help people who were helpless to help themselves. What money I earned I gave away; when I couldn't give a man a job myself I went to my friends and begged them to give a man the work he needed. I brought them home and fed them; I fixed them up on the floor when the beds were full. I got hell all around for doing too much and neglecting my own wife and child. My boss looked upon me as a fool, and instead of praising me for my efforts bawled hell out of me continually. I was always between two fires, from above and from below. I saw finally that no matter how much I did it was just a drop in the bucket. I'm not saying that I grew indifferent or hardened. No, but I realized that it would take a revolution to make any appreciable change in conditions. And when I say a revolution I mean a real revolution, something far more radical and sweeping than the Russian revolution, for instance. I still think that, but I don't think it can be done politically or economically. Governments can't bring it about. Only individuals, each one working in his own quiet way. It must be a revolution of the heart. Our attitude towards life has to be fundamentally altered. We've got to advance to another level, a level from which we can take in the whole earth with one glance. We have to have a vision of the globe, including all the people who inhabit it—down to the lowest and the most primitive man.

"To come back to our friend. . . . I wasn't too unkind to him, was I? You know damned well I've never refused a man help when he asked for it. But he didn't want help. He wanted sympathy. He wanted us to try to dissuade him from accomplishing his own destruction. And when he had melted us with his heartbreaking stories he wanted to have the pleasure of saying no and leaving us high and dry. He gets a kick out of that. A quiet sort of revenge, as it were, for his inability to cure himself of his sorrows. I figure it doesn't help a man any to encourage him in that direction. If a woman gets hysterical you know that the best thing to do is to slap her face good and hard. The same with these poor devils: they've got to be made to understand that they are not the only ones in the world who are suffering. They make a vice of their suffering. An analyst might cure him—and again he might not. And in any case, how would you get him to the analyst? If I hadn't been so tired, and if I had had more money, I'd have tried another line with him. I'd have bought him some booze—not just a bottle, but a case of whiskey, two cases or three, if I were able to afford it. I tried that once on a friend of mine—another confirmed drunkard. Do you know, he was so damned furious when he saw all that liquor that he never opened a single bottle. He was insulted, so he pretended. It didn't faze me in the least. I had gotten rather fed up with his antics. When he was sober he was a prince, but when he got drunk he was just impossible. Well, thereafter, every time he came to see me, as soon as he suggested a little drink, I poured out a half dozen glasses at once for him. While he was debating whether to touch it or not I would excuse myself and run out to buy more. It worked—in his case, at least. It cost me his friendship, to be sure, but it stopped him from playing the drunkard with me. They've tried similar things in certain prisons I know of. They don't force a man to work, if he doesn't want to. On the contrary, they give him a comfortable cell, plenty to eat, cigars, cigarettes, wine or beer, according to his taste, a servant to wait on him, anything he wants save his freedom. After a few days of it the fellow usually begs to be permitted to work. A man just can't stand having too much of a good thing. Give a man all he wants and more and you'll cure him of his appetites in nine cases out of ten. It's so damned simple—it's strange we don't take advantage of such ideas."

When I had crawled into bed and turned out the light I found that I was wide awake. Often, when I've listened to a man for a whole evening, turning myself into a receiving station, I lie awake and rehearse the man's story from beginning to end. I like to see how accurately I can retrace the innumerable incidents which a man can relate in the course of several hours, especially if he is given free rein. I almost always think of such talks as a big tree with limbs and branches and leaves and buds. Roots, too, which have their grip in the common soil of human experience and which make any story, no matter how fantastic or incredible, quite plausible, provided you give the man the time and attention he demands. The most wonderful thing, to carry the image further, is the buds: these are the little incidents which like seeds a man will often plant in your mind to blossom later when the memory of him is almost lost. Some men are particularly skillful in handling these buds; they actually seem to possess the power to graft them on to your own story-telling tree so that when they blossom forth you imagine that they were your own, though you never cease marveling that your own little brain could have produced such astonishing fruit.

As I say, I was turning it all over in my mind and chuckling to myself to think how clever I was to have detected certain definite falsifications, certain distortions and omissions which, when one is listening intently, one seldom catches. Presently I recalled how he had admitted some slight fabrications only to emphasize that the rest of his yarn was pure wool. At this point I chuckled aloud. Rattner was tossing about, evidently no more able than I to close his eyes.

"Are you still awake?" I asked quietly.

He gave a grunt.

"Listen," I said, "there's one thing I want to ask you— do you belive he was telling the truth about himself?"

Rattner, too tired I suppose to go into any subtleties of analysis, began to hem and haw. In the main he thought the fellow had been telling us the truth. *"Why,* didn't you believe him?" he asked.

"You remember," I said, "when I touched him to the quick . . . you remember how sincerely he spoke? Well, it was at that moment that I doubted him. At that moment he told us the biggest lie of all—when he said that the rest was all true. I don't believe that any of it was true, not even the story about knowing your friend. You remember how quickly he married him off to his sister? That was sheer spontaneous invention. I was tracing it all back just now. And I remembered very distinctly how, when you were discussing your friend the architect, he always told his part after you had made a few remarks. He was getting his clue from you all the time. He's very agile and he's certainly fertile, I'll say that for him, but I don't believe a damned thing he told us, except perhaps that he was in the army and got badly bunged up. Even that, of course, could have been trumped up. Did you ever feel a head that was trepanned? That seems like solid fact, of course, and yet somehow, I don't know just why, I could doubt even what my fingers told me. When a man has an inventive brain like his he could tell you anything and make it sound convincing. Mind you, it doesn't make his story any less real, as far as I'm concerned. Whether all those things happened or not, they're true just the same. A minute ago, when I was mulling it over to myself, I caught myself deforming certain incidents, certain remarks he made, in order to make the story a better story. Not to make it more truthful, but more true, if you see the difference. I had it all figured out, how I would tell it myself, if I ever got down to it. . . ."

Rattner began to protest that I was too sweeping in my judgment, which only served to remind me of the marvelous poem he had recited for us.

"I say," I began again, "what would you think if I told you that the poem which he got off with such gusto was somebody else's? Would that shock you?"

"You mean you recognized it—you had heard it before?"

"No, I don't mean to say that, but I'm damned sure he was not the author of it. Why did he talk about his unusual memory immediately afterwards—didn't that strike you as rather strange? He could have spoken about a thousand things, but no, he had to speak of that. Besides, he recited it too well. Poets aren't usually so good at reciting their own things. Very few poets remember their verses, particularly if they're long ones such as his was. To recite a poem with such feeling a man has to admire it greatly and a poet, once he's written a poem out, forgets it. In any case, he wouldn't be going around spouting it aloud to every Tom, Dick and Harry he meets. A bad poet might, but then that poem wasn't written by a bad poet. And furthermore, a poem like that couldn't have been written by a man like our friend who boasted so glibly about turning out crap for the magazines whenever he needed to earn an honest or a dishonest penny. No, he memorized that poem because it was just the sort of thing he would like to have written himself and couldn't. I'm sure of it."

"There's something to what you say there," said Rattner sleepily. He sighed and turned over, his face towards the wall. In a jiffy he had turned round again and was sitting bolt upright.

"What's the matter," I asked, "what hit you?"

"Why my friend what's his name . . . you know, the architect who was my buddy. *Who* mentioned his name first—*he* did, didn't he? Well, how could be he lying then?"

"That's easy," I said. "Your friend's name is known to millions of people. He selected it just because it was a well-known name; he thought it would add tone to his story. That was when he was talking about his inventions, you remember? He just made a stab in the dark—and happened to strike your friend."

"He seemed to know a hell of a lot about him," said Rattner, still unconvinced.

"Well, don't you know lots of things about people whom you've never met? Why, if a man is any kind of celebrity we often know more about him than he does himself. Besides, this bird may have run into him at a bar some time or other. What sounded fishy to me was marrying him off to his sister right away."

"Yep, he was taking a big chance there," said Rattner, "knowing that I had been such an intimate friend."

"But you had already told him you hadn't seen each other since you were buddies together, don't forget that. Why he could have given him not only a wife but a half dozen children besides—you wouldn't be able to disprove it. Anyway, that's one thing we can check up on. I do wish you'd write to your friend and see if he knows this guy or not."

"You bet I will," said Rattner, getting out of bed at once and looking for his notebook. "You've got me all worked up about it now. Jesus, what licks me is that you could have entertained such suspicions and listened to him the way you did. You looked at him as though he were handing you the Gospel. I didn't know you were such an actor."

"I'm not," I hastened to put in. "At the time I really believed every word he was telling us. Or, to be more exact, I never stopped to think whether what he was saying was so or not so. When a story is good I listen, and if it develops afterwards that it was a lie why so much the better—I like a good lie just as much as the truth. A story is a story, whether it's based on fact or fancy."

"Now I'd like to ask you a question," Rattner put in. "Why do you suppose he was so sore at Roosevelt?"

"I don't think he was half so sore as he pretended to be," I answered promptly. "I think his sole motive for introducing Roosevelt's name was to get us to listen to that scurrilous poem he had cooked up. You noticed, I hope, that there was no comparison between the two poems. *He* wrote the one on Roosevelt, that I'm positive of. Only a bar-fly could cook up such ingenious nonsense. He probably hasn't anything against Roosevelt. He wanted us to admire the poem and then, failing to get a reaction from us, he got his wires crossed and connected Roosevelt with Woodrow Wilson, the demon who sent him to hell."

"He certainly had a vicious look when he was talking about the war," said Rattner. "I don't doubt him for a minute when he said he had murdered plenty of men. I wouldn't want to run across him in the dark when he was in a bad mood."

"Yes, there I agree with you," I said. "I think the reason he was so bitter about killing was that he was a killer himself. . . . I was almost going to say a killer by nature, but I take that back. What I do think, though, is that the experience in the trenches often brings out the killer in a man. We're all killers, only most of us never get a chance to cultivate the germ. The worst killers, of course, are the ones who stay at home. They can't help it, either. The soldier gets a chance to vent his feelings, but the man who stays at home has no outlet for his passions. They ought to kill off the newspaper men right at the start, that's my idea. Those are the men who inspire the killing. Hitler is a pure, clean-hearted idealist compared to those birds. I don't mean the correspondents. I mean the editors and the stuffed shirts who order the editors to write the poison that they hand out."

"You know," said Rattner, in a soft, reflective voice, "there was only one man I felt like killing when I was in the service—and that was the lieutenant, the second-lieutenant, of our company."

"Don't tell me," I said. "I've heard that same story a thousand times. And it's always a lieutenant. Nobody with any self-respect wants to be a lieutenant. They all have inferiority complexes. Many of them get shot in the back, I'm told."

"Worse than that sometimes," said Rattner. "This chap I'm telling you about, why I can't imagine anyone being hated more than he was—not only by us but by his superiors. The officers loathed him. Anyway, let me finish telling you about him. . . . You see, when we were finally demobilized everybody was gunning for him. I knew some fellows who came all the way to New York from Texas and California to look him up and take a poke at him. And when I say a poke I don't mean just a poke—I mean to beat the piss out of him. I don't know whether it's true or not, but the story I heard later on was this, that he was beaten up so often and so badly that finally he changed his name and moved to another state. You can imagine what what's his name would have done to a guy like that, can't you? I don't think he'd have bothered to soil his hands. I think he'd have plugged him or else cracked him over the head with a bottle. And if he'd have had to swing for it I don't think he would have batted an eyelash. Did you notice how smoothly he passed over that story about cracking a friend with a broken bottle? He told it as though it were incidental to something else—it rang true to me. If it had been a lie he would have made more of it. But he told it as though he were neither ashamed nor proud of doing what he did. He was just giving us the facts, that's all."

I lay on my back, when we had ceased talking, with eyes wide open, staring at the ceiling. Certain phrases which our friend had dropped returned obsessively to plague me. The collection of vice-presidents of the United States, which he had so accurately described, was a most persistent image. I was trying my damnedest to recall in what town I too had seen this collection in a drugstore window. Chattanooga, most likely. And yet it couldn't have been Chattanooga either, because in the same window there was a large photograph of Lincoln. I remembered how my eye had flitted back and forth from the rogues' gallery of vice-presidents to the portrait of Lincoln's wife. I had felt terribly sorry for Lincoln at that moment, not because he had been assassinated but because he had been saddled with that crazy bitch of a wife who almost drove him insane. Yes, as the woman from Georgia had said, we *were* trying to make a *he*-ro of him. And yet for all the good he had tried to do he had caused a lot of harm. He almost wrecked the country. As for Lee, on the other hand, there was no division of opinion throughout the country as to the greatness of his soul. As time goes on the North becomes more enamored of him. . . . *The killing* —that's what I couldn't fathom. What had it accomplished? I wondered if our friend had really gone up to the circle and held communion with the spirit of the man he revered. And then what? Then he had gone to a cheap lodging house and fought with the bed bugs until dawn, was that it? And the next day and the day after? Legions of them floating around. And me priding myself on my detective ability, getting all worked up because I uncovered a few flaws in his story. A revolution of the heart! Fine phrase, that, but meanwhile I'm lying comfortably between clean warm sheets. I'm lying here making emendations in his story so that when I come to put it down on paper it will sound more authentic than the authentic one. Trying to kid myself that if I tell the story real well perhaps it will make people more kindly and tolerant towards such poor devils. Rot! All rot! There are the people who give and forgive without stint, without question, and there are the other kind who always know how to muster a thousand reasons for withholding their aid. The latter never graduate into the former class. Never. The gulf between them is as wide as hell. One is born kind, indulgent, forgiving, tolerant, merciful. One isn't made that way through religion or education. Carry it out to the year 56,927 A.D. and still there will be the two classes of men. And between the two there will always be a shadow world, the world of ghostly creatures who toss about in vain, walking the streets in torment while the world sleeps. . . .

It wasn't so long ago that I was walking in that same shadow world myself. I used to walk around in the dead of night begging for coppers so that I could fill my empty belly. And one night in the rain, walking with head down and full of nothing but misery, I run plump into a man with a cape and an opera hat and in a faint, cheerless voice I beg in my customary way for a few pence. And without stopping, without even looking at me, the man from the opera digs in his vest pocket, pulls out a handful of change and flings it at me. The money rolls all over the sidewalk and into the gutter. Suddenly I straightened up, stiff and taut with anger. Suddenly I was completely out of the come, snorting like a bull and ready to charge. I waved my fist and shouted in the direction the man had taken, but there was no sight or sound of him. He had vanished as mysteriously as he had appeared. I stood there a moment or so undecided what to do, whether to run after him and vent my spleen or quietly set about searching for the shower of coins he had flung at me. Presently I was laughing hysterically. Run after him, bawl him out, challenge him to a duel? Why, he wouldn't even recognize me! I was a nonentity to him, just a voice in the dark asking for alms. I drew myself up still more erect and took a deep breath. I looked around calmly and deliberately. The street was empty, not even a cab rolling along. I felt strong and chastened, as if I had just taken a whipping I deserved. "You bastard," I said aloud, looking in the direction of my invisible benefactor, "I'm going to thank you for this! You don't know what you've done for me. Yes sir, I want to thank you from the bottom of my heart. I'm cured." And laughing quietly, trembling with thanksgiving, I got down on my hands and knees in the rain and began raking in the wet coins. Those which had rolled into the gutter were covered with mud. I washed them carefully in a little pool of rain water near a post of the elevated line. Then I counted them slowly and deliciously. Thirty-six cents altogether. A tidy sum. The cellar where we lived was near by. I brought the bright clean coins home to my wife and showed them to her triumphantly. She looked at me as if I had gone out of my head.

"Why did you wash them?" she said nervously.

"Because they had fallen in the gutter," I answered. "An angel with an opera hat left them there for me. He was in too much of a hurry to pick them up for me. . . ."

"Are you sure you're all right?" said my wife, eyeing me anxiously.

"I never felt better in my life," I said. "I've just been humiliated, beaten, dragged in the mud and washed in the blood of the Lamb. I'm hungry, are you? Let's eat."

And so at 3:10 of an Easter morning we sallied forth from the dungeon arm in arm and ordered two hamburgers and coffee at the greasy spoon cafeteria on Myrtle Avenue corner of Fulton Street. I was never so wide awake in my life, and after I had offered up a short prayer to St. Anthony I made a vow to remain wide awake and if possible to wake up the whole world, saying in conclusion Amen! and wiping my mouth with a paper napkin.

Via Dieppe-Newhaven

THE THING WAS that I wanted to be among English-speaking people again, for a little while at least. I had nothing against the French; on the contrary, I had at last made a bit of a home for myself in Clichy and everything would have been swell if it hadn't been for the fact that I had just gone through a crisis with my wife. She was living in Montparnasse and I was living with my friend Fred, who had taken an apartment, in Clichy just outside the Porte. We had agreed to separate; she was going back to America as soon as the money arrived for the boat fare.

So far so good. I had said good-bye to her and I thought
everything was finished. Then one day when I walked into
the grocer's the old woman informed me that my wife had
just been in with a young man and that they had taken
away a good supply of groceries which they had charged
up to my account. The old woman seemed a bit perplexed
and a little worried too. I told her it was O. K. And it was
O. K. too, because I knew my wife didn't have any money,
and after all a wife has to eat just like any other person.
About the young man, that was O. K. too; he was just a
fairy who felt sorry for her and I supposed he had put her
up for the time being in his apartment. In fact, everything
was O. K. except that she was still in Paris, and when in
Christ's name was she going to beat it, that's what I was
wondering about.

A few more days passed and then she dropped in one
late afternoon to have dinner with us. Why not? We could
always scrape up a bit of food whereas in Montparnasse,
among the riff-raff she was obliged to hang out with, food
was almost unobtainable. After the dinner she got hysterical: she said she was suffering from dysentery ever since
she had left me and that it was my fault, that I had tried
to poison her. I walked her to the Metro station at the
Porte without saying a word. I was sore as hell, so god-
damned sore that I couldn't talk. She was sore too, sore
because I refused to argue the matter with her. I thought
to myself, walking back, well this is the last straw, she
surely won't come back again. I poisoned her. Good, if
she wants to think that way let her! That ought to settle
the issue.

A few days later I had a letter from her asking for a
little cash with which to meet the rent. Seems she wasn't
living with the fairy at all, but in a cheap hotel back of the
Gare Montparnasse. I couldn't give her the money immediately as I didn't have any myself so I let a few days in-
tervene before going to her hotel and settling the bill.
While I was trotting round to her hotel a pneumatique had
come for me saying that she simply must have the money
or she'd be kicked out. If I had had a little money I
wouldn't have put her to all these humiliations, but the
point is I didn't have any. However, she didn't believe me.

And even if it were true, she said, I could at least have borrowed it for her. Which was also true. But I was never good on borrowing large sums; all my life I had been used to asking for hand-outs, for chicken feed, and feeling damned grateful when I got that. She seemed to have forgotten that. It was natural enough that she should because she was bitter and her pride had been wounded. And to do her justice I must add that had the situation been reversed the money would have been forthcoming; she always knew how to raise money for me but never for herself. That I've got to admit.

I was getting pretty wrought up about the whole thing. I felt like a louse. And the worse I felt the less I was able to do. I even suggested that she come back and stay with us until the money which she was expecting for the boat trip should come. But this she wouldn't hear of, naturally. Or was it natural? I was so damned perplexed and humiliated and confused that I didn't know any more what was natural and what wasn't. Money. Money. All my life it had been a question of money. I would never be able to solve the problem and I didn't hope to.

After turning round and round like a rat in a trap I got the brilliant idea of beating it myself. Just walk out on the problem, that's always the easiest way. I don't know how the idea came to me but suddenly I had decided that I would go to London. If you had offered me a chateau in Touraine I would have said no. For some reason or other I had made up my mind that it must be London and no other place. The reason I gave myself was that she'd never think of looking for me in London. She knew I hated the place. But the real reason, as I soon discovered, was that I wanted to be among English-speaking people; I wanted to hear English spoken twenty-four hours of the day, and nothing but English. In my weak condition that was like falling back on the bosom of the Lord. Talking and listening to English meant just that less strain. God knows, when you're in a jam, to talk a foreign language or even just to listen to it—because you can't shut your ears even if you try to—is a subtle form of torture. I had absolutely nothing against the French, nor against the language they spoke. Up until she arrived on the scene I had been living in a sort of Paradise. Suddenly everything had gone sour. I found myself muttering things against the French, and against the language particularly, which I would never have dreamed of thinking in my sober senses. I knew it was my own fault, but that only made it worse. Well, London then. A little vacation and perhaps by the time I returned she would have left. That's all there was to it.

I rustled up the dough for a visa and a return trip ticket. I bought a visa for a year thinking that if by chance I should change my mind about the English I might go back a second or a third time to England. It was getting on towards Christmas and I began to think what a jolly old place London might be during the holidays. Perhaps I would find a different sort of London than the one I knew, a Dickensian London such as tourists always dream of. I had the visa and the ticket in my pocket and just about enough dough to last me for ten days. I was feeling almost jubilant about the trip.

When I got back to Clichy it was almost dinner time. I walked into the kitchen and there was my wife helping Fred with the dinner. They were laughing and joking as I walked in. I knew that Fred wouldn't say anything to her about my going to London and so I sat down to the table and laughed and joked a bit myself. It was a jolly meal, I must say, and everything would have gone off splendidly if Fred hadn't been obliged to go to the newspaper office after dinner. I had been canned a few weeks ago but he was still working, though expecting the same fate any day. The reason I was canned was that, even though I was an American, I had no right to be working on an American newspaper as a proof-reader. According to French theory the job could just as well have been held by a Frenchman who knew English. That griped me a bit and no doubt contributed to my feeling sour towards the French the last few weeks. Anyway, that was over and done with and I was a free man again and I would soon be in London talking English all day long and far into the night if I wanted to. Besides, my book was coming out very soon and that might change everything. All in all things weren't half as black as they had seemed a few days back. Thinking how nicely I was going to duck the whole thing I got a bit careless and ran out, in a moment of exuberation, to buy a bottle of Chartreuse which I knew she liked better than anything. That was a fatal mistake. The Chartreuse made her mellow and then hysterical and then reproving. We sat there at the table, the two of us, and I guess we rehearsed a lot of things that should have been forgotten. Finally I got to such a point of guilt and tenderness that I blurted out the whole thing—about the trip to London, the money I had borrowed, and so on and so forth. I forked the whole thing out and laid it on the table. There it was, I don't know how many pounds and shillings, all in bright new English money. I told her I was sorry and to hell with the trip and to-morrow I would try to get a refund on the tickets and give that to her too.

And here again I must render her justice. She really didn't want to take the money. It made her wince, I could see that, but finally she accepted it reluctantly and stuffed it away in her bag. As she was leaving she forgot the bag and I was obliged to run down the stairs after her and hand it to her. As she took the bag she said good-bye again and this time I felt that it was the last good-bye. She said good-bye and she stood there on the stairs looking up at me with a strange sorrowful smile. If I had made the least gesture I know she would have thrown the money out of the window and rushed back into my arms and stayed with me forever. I took a long look at her, walked slowly back to the door, and closed it. I went back to the kitchen table, sat there a few minutes looking at the empty glasses, and then I broke down and sobbed like a child.

It was about three in the morning when Fred came back from work. He saw right away that something had gone wrong. I told him what had happened and then we sat down and ate, and after we had eaten we drank some good Algerian wine and then some Chartreuse and after that a little cognac. It was a damned shame, in Fred's opinion, and I was a fool to have forked up all the money. I agreed, but I felt good about it just the same.

"And what about London? Do you mean to tell me you're not going to London?" he says.

"No," I said, "I've given up the idea. Besides, I couldn't

go now even if I wanted to. Where's the dough to come from?"

Fred didn't seem to think the lack of dough was any grave obstacle. He thought he could borrow a couple of hundred francs at the office and on pay-day, which was only a few days off, he would wire me more. We sat there discussing the thing until dawn, and of course drinking a bit too. When I hit the hay I could hear the Westminster chimes—and a few rusty sleigh bells too. I saw a beautiful blanket of snow lying over dirty London and everybody greeting me with a hearty "Merry Christmas!"—*in English,* to be sure.

I made the Channel crossing at night. It was a miserable night and we stayed indoors shivering with the cold. I had a hundred franc note and some change—that was all. The idea was that as soon as I found a hotel I was to cable and Fred would cable back some dough. I sat at the long table in the salon listening to the conversation going on around me. The thought uppermost in my mind was how to make the hundred francs stretch as far as possible, because the more I thought about it the less sure I was that Fred would raise the dough immediately. The scraps of conversation I picked up also had to do with money. Money. Money. The same thing everywhere and all the time. It seems that England had just that day paid her debt to America, much against her will. She had kept her word, as they were saying all about me. England always kept her word. And more of that and more, until I felt like strangling them for their bloody honesty.

I hadn't intended to break the hundred franc note until absolutely necessary, but with this silly conversation going on about England keeping her word and knowing that they had spotted me as an American I finally got so jumpy that I ordered a beer and a ham sandwich. That brought me directly into contact with the steward. He wanted to know what I thought about the situation. I could see that he thought it was a bloody crime what we had done to England. I felt sore that he should make me responsible for the situation just because I happened to be born an American. So I told him I didn't know anything about the situation, that it was none of my affair, and furthermore that it was a matter of absolute indifference to me whether England paid her debts or didn't pay her debts. He didn't relish this very much. A man ought to have an interest in the affairs of his country, even if his country is in the wrong, that's what he thought. I told him I didn't give a damn about America or Americans. I told him I didn't have an ounce of patriotism in me. At that moment a man who had been pacing up and down beside the table stopped to listen to me. I had a feeling that he was a spy or a detective. I piped down almost at once and turned to the young man beside me who had also called for a beer and a sandwich.

Apparently he had been listening to me with some interest. He wanted to know where I came from and what I was going to do in England. I told him I was taking a little vacation, and then, impulsively, I asked him if he could recommend a very cheap hotel. He said he had been away from England for quite a long while and that he didn't know London very well anyhow. Said he had been living in Australia the last few years. Just then the steward happened along and the young man interrupted himself to ask the steward if he knew of any good cheap little hotel in London. The steward called the waiter over and asked him the same question, and just as he put the question to the waiter the man who looked like a spy came along and paused a moment to listen in. From the serious way in which the subject was discussed I could see at once that I had made a mistake. One shouldn't ask questions like that of a steward or a waiter. I felt that they were looking me over suspiciously, that they were giving my pocket-book the X-ray. I tossed off the beer at one gulp and, as though to prove that money was the least of my worries I called for another and then, turning to the young man at my elbow, I asked him if he wouldn't let me buy him a drink too. When the steward came back with the drinks we were deep in the wilds of Australia. He started to say something about a hotel but I told him immediately to forget it. It was just an idle question, I added. That seemed to stump him. He stood there a few moments not knowing what to do, then suddenly, moved by some friendly impulse, he blurted out that he would be glad to

put me up in his own home at Newhaven if I cared to
spend the night there. I thanked him warmly and told
him not to worry about it any more, that I would go on
to London just the same. It really isn't important, I added.
And the moment I said it I knew that that too was a mistake, because somehow, despite myself, I had made the
thing seem quite important to everybody.

There was still a bit of time to kill and so I listened to
the young Englishman who had had a strange time of it
in Australia. He was telling of his life as a sheep herder,
how they castrated I don't know how many thousands of
sheep in a day. One had to work fast. So fast, in fact, that
the most expedient thing to do was to grab the testicles
with your teeth and then a quick slit with the knife and
spit them out. He was trying to estimate how many thousand pairs of testicles he had bitten off in this hand to
mouth operation during his sojourn in Australia. And as
he was going through his mental calculations he wiped his
mouth with the back of his hand.

"You must have had a strange taste in your mouth," I
said, instinctively wiping my own mouth.

"It wasn't as bad as you might imagine," he answered
calmly. "You get used to everything—in time. No, it
wasn't a bad taste at all . . . the idea is worse than the
actual thing. Just the same, I never thought when I left
my comfortable home in England that I would be spitting
out those things for a living. A man can get used to doing
most anything when he's really up against it."

I was thinking the same thing. I was thinking of the
time I burned brush in an orange grove in Chula Vista.
Ten hours a day in the broiling sun running from one fire
to another and the flies biting like mad. And for what?
To prove to myself that I was a man, I suppose, that I
could take it on the chin. And another time working as a
gravedigger: to show that I wasn't afraid of tackling anything. The gravedigger! With a volume of Nietzsche under
his arm, and trying to memorize the last part of Faust to
and from work. Well, as the steward says, *"the English
never twist you!"* The boat is coming to a stop. Another
swig of beer to drown the taste of sheep's nuts and a
handsome little tip for the waiter just to prove that Ameri-

cans pay their debts too sometimes. In the excitement I find myself quite alone, standing behind a bulky Englishman with a checkered cap and a big ulster. Landing in any other country the checkered cap would look ridiculous, but as it's his own country he can do as he pleases, and what's more I almost admire him for it, it makes him seem so big and independent. I'm beginning to think that they're not such a bad race after all.

On deck it's dark and drizzly. The last time I pulled into England, that was coming up the Thames, it was also dark and drizzly and the faces were ashen gray and uniforms were black and the houses were grim and grimy. And up High Holborn Street every morning I remember there passed me the most respectable, lamentable, dilapidated paupers God ever made. Gray, watery paupers with bowlers and cutaways and that absurd air of respectability which only the English can muster in adversity. And now the language is coming to me a little stronger and I must say I don't like it at all: it sounds oily, slimy, servile, unctuous. I feel the class line cutting through the accents. The man with the checkered cap and the ulster has suddenly become a pompous ass; he seems to be talking Choctaw to the porters. I hear Sir all the time. Can I do this, *Sir?* Which way, *Sir?* Yes, *Sir.* No, *Sir.* Bugger me if it doesn't make me a bit creepy, all this yes sir and no sir, *Sir my ass,* I say under my breath.

At the Immigration Office. Waiting my turn on the line. The rich bastards go first, as usual. We move up inch by inch. Those who've passed through are having their baggage inspected on the quay. The porters are bustling about loaded down like donkeys. Only two people ahead of me now. I have my passport in my hand and my train ticket and my baggage checks. Now I'm standing square in front of him, offering him my passport. He looks at the big white sheet beside him, finds my name and checks it off.

"How long do you intend to stay in England, Mr. Miller?" he says, holding the passport in his hand as though ready to give it back to me.

"A week or two," I answer.

"You're going to London, are you?"

"Yes."

"What hotel are you stopping at, Mr. Miller?"

I have to smile at this. "Why, I don't know," I respond, still smiling. "Perhaps you can recommend me a hotel."

"Have you any friends in London, Mr. Miller?"

"No."

"Just what are you going to do in London, if I may ask?"

"Why, I'm going to take a little vacation." Still smiling.

"I suppose you have enough money for your stay in England?"

"I think so," says I, still nonchalant, still smiling. And thinking to myself what a cinch it is to bluff it through with questions like that.

"Do you mind showing me your money, Mr. Miller?"

"Of course not," and reaching into my jeans I haul out the remains of the hundred franc note. The people next to me are laughing. I try to laugh too, but I'm not very successful. As for my inquisitor, he gives a feeble little chuckle and looking me square in the eyes he says with all the sarcasm he can put into it: "You didn't expect to stay very long in London on that, did you, Mr. Miller?"

Always this *Mr. Miller* tacked on to every phrase! I'm beginning to dislike the son-of-a-bitch. What's more it's beginning to get uncomfortable.

"Look here," I say, still amiable and still outwardly nonchalant, "I don't intend to have a vacation on that. As soon as I get a hotel I expect to wire for money. I left Paris in a great hurry and . . ."

He cuts me short. Can I give him the name of my bank in Paris, he wants to know.

"I haven't got a bank account," I'm obliged to answer. That makes a very bad impression I realize at once. I can feel the hostility growing up all about me. People who were holding their bags are putting them down now, as though they knew they were in for a long siege. The passport which he had been holding in his hands like a little testament he puts on the counter before him and holds it there, like a damaging piece of evidence, with outstretched finger-tips.

"Where were you going to get the money from, Mr. Miller?" he asks more blandly than ever.

"Why, from a friend of mine, the man who lives with me in Paris."

"Has he a bank account?"

"No, but he's got a job. He works on the Chicago Tribune."

"And you think he will send you the money for your vacation?"

"I don't think so, *I know so,*" I answered tartly. "I'm not trying to give you a cock and bull story. I told you I left in a hurry. I left with the understanding that he'd send me the money as soon as I arrived in London. Besides, it's *my money,* not his."

"You left your money with him rather than put it in a bank, is that it, Mr. Miller?"

"Well," I said, beginning to lose my temper, "it isn't a hell of a lot of money and besides, I don't see the point of all this. If you don't believe me I'll stay right here and you can send a cable and find out for yourself."

"Just a minute, Mr. Miller. You say the two of you live together . . . do you live in a hotel or in an apartment?"

"An apartment."

"And the apartment is in your name?"

"No, in his. That is, it belongs to the both of us, but it's in his name because he's a Frenchman and it makes it easier."

"And he keeps your money for you?"

"No, not usually. You see, I left under rather unusual circumstances. I . . ."

"Just a minute, Mr. Miller," and he motions to me to step back from the ranks a bit. At the same time he calls one of his assistants over and hands him my passport. The latter takes the passport and goes behind a screen some distance off. I stand there watching the others go through.

"You might go and have your baggage inspected meanwhile," I hear him say as if in a trance. I move off to the shed and open my luggage. The train is waiting for us. It looks like a team of Eskimo dogs straining at the leash. The locomotive is puffing and steaming. Finally I walk back and take my stand in front of my interlocutor. The last few passengers are being hustled through the examination.

Now the tall thin man from behind the screen comes forward with the passport in his hand. He seems determined in advance that I'm a malefactor.

"You're an American citizen, Mr. Miller?"

"Obviously," I answer. With this guy I know there's going to be no mercy. He hasn't a speck of humor in him.

"How long have you been in France?"

"Two or three years, I guess. You can see the date there for yourself . . . *Why?* What's that got to do with it?

"You were thinking of spending several months in England, were you?"

"No, I wasn't. I was thinking of spending a week or ten days there, that's all. But now . . ."

"So you bought a visa for a year, thinking to spend a week."

"I bought a return trip ticket too, if that interests you."

"One could always throw the return ticket away," he says with a malicious twist of the mouth.

"One could if he were an idiot. I don't get the point. And anyway, look here, I'm tired of all this nonsense. I'm going to stay in Newhaven overnight and take the next boat back. I don't have to spend my vacation in England."

"Not so fast, Mr. Miller. I think we ought to look into this a little more closely."

As he said this I heard the whistle blow. The passengers were all aboard and the train was just starting. I thought of my trunk which I had checked through to London. Nearly all my manuscripts were in it, and my typewriter too. A nice mess, I thought to myself. All because of that chicken feed I slapped down on the counter.

The little fat fellow with the bland imperturbable mask now joined us. He seemed to be expecting a treat.

Hearing the train roll out of the station I resigned myself to the inquisition. Thinks I to myself, now that they've * * * * * me, let's see how far they can prolong the agony. First of all, however, I demanded my passport back. If they wanted to grill me a little more O. K. There was nothing to do at that hour of the night and before turning in at Newhaven I thought I'd go through with the song and dance.

To my amazement the tall thin fellow refused to return

my passport. That made me furious. I demanded to know
if there was an American Consul on hand. "Listen," I said,
"you may think what you like, but that passport belongs
to me and I want it back."

"There's no need to get excited, Mr. Miller. You'll have
your passport before you leave. But first there are a few
questions I'd like to put to you . . . I see that you are a
married man. Is your wife living with you—and your
friend? Or is she in America?"

"I don't see that that's any of your business," I said.
"But since you brought the subject up I'm going to tell you
something now. The reason I came away with so little
money is because I gave the money for my trip to my wife
before leaving. We're separating and she's going back to
America in a few days. I gave her the money because she
was broke."

"How much money did you give her, if I may ask?"

"You're asking so damned many questions that you
have no right to ask I don't see why you shouldn't ask that
too. If you want to know, I gave her about 60 pounds.
Let's see. I may still have the exchange slip in my wallet . . ." And I made a gesture as if to reach for my wallet
and look for the slip.

"Wasn't that rather foolish to give your wife all that
money and come to England penniless, or almost so?"

I gave him a sour smile. "My dear man, I've tried to explain to you that I'm not coming to England as a pauper.
If you had let me go to London and wire for the money
everything would have been all right. I suppose it's a waste
of time to say a thing like this to you but try to understand
me, will you? *I'm a writer*. I do things impulsively. I don't
have bank accounts and I don't plan things years in advance. When I want to do something I do it. For some
reason or other you seem to think that I want to come to
England to . . . frankly, I don't know what the hell's in
your mind. I just wanted to come to England to hear English, if you can believe it—and partly too to escape my
wife. Does that make sense to you?"

"I should say it does," says the tall thin fellow. "You
want to run away from your wife and let her become a
public charge. How do you know she won't follow you to

England? And how will you take care of her in England—without money?"

I felt as though I were talking to a stone wall. What was the use of rehearsing the whole thing again? "Listen," I said, "as far as I'm concerned I don't care what happens to her. If she becomes a public charge that's her affair, not mine."

"You're working for the Chicago Tribune, you say?"

"I never said anything of the kind. I said my friend, the man who was to send me the money, *he's* working on the Chicago Tribune."

"You never worked for the newspaper then?"

"Yes, I used to work for them, but I don't now. They fired me a few weeks ago."

He snapped me up immediately. "Oh, then you *did* work for the newspaper in Paris?"

"Didn't I just say so? Why? Why do you ask?"

"Mr. Miller, could I see your carte d'identité . . . I suppose you *have* a carte d'identité, living in Paris, as you say."

I fished it out for him. The two of them looked it over together.

"You have a non-worker's card—yet you worked for the Chicago Tribune as a proof-reader. How do you explain that, Mr. Miller?"

"No, I suppose I can't explain that to you. I suppose it's useless to explain to you that I'm an American citizen and that the Chicago Tribune is an American newspaper and that therefore . . ."

"Excuse me, but why were you dismissed from the newspaper?"

"That's just what I was coming to. You see, the French officials, those who have to do with the red tape, seem to take the same attitude as you do. Perhaps I could have remained on the Tribune if I hadn't also been a bad proof-reader. That's the real reason why I was fired, if you want to know."

"You seem rather proud of the fact."

"I am. I think it's a mark of intelligence."

"And so, not having a job on the Tribune any more you thought you'd come to England for a little vacation. And you provided yourself with a visa for a year and a return trip ticket."

"Also to hear English and to escape my wife," I added.

Here the little round-faced fellow spoke up. The tall fellow seemed ready to relinquish the tussle.

"You're a writer, Mr. Miller?"

"Yes."

"You mean you write books and stories?"

"Yes."

"Do you write for the magazines in America?"

"Yes."

"Which ones . . . can you name a few?"

"Certainly. The American Mercury, Harper's, Atlantic Monthly, Scribner's, the Virginia Quarterly, The Yale Review . . ."

"Just a minute." He walked back to the counter and bending down he pulled out a big fat directory. "American Mercury . . . American Mercury . . ." he kept mumbling as he thumbed the pages. "Henry V. Miller, isn't it? Henry V. Miller . . . Henry V. Miller . . . Was it this year or last year, Mr. Miller?"

"It may be three years ago—*for the Mercury*," I said blandly.

Apparently he had no book on hand that went back that far. Couldn't I give him the name of a magazine I had written for in the last year or two? I said no, I had been too busy writing a book the last year or so.

Had the book been published? What was the name of the American publisher?

I said it had been published by an Englishman.

What was the name of the publisher?

"The Obelisk Press."

He scratched his head. "An *English* publisher?" He couldn't seem to remember any English house by that name. He called his side-kick who had disappeared behind the screen with my passport. "Ever hear of the Obelisk Press?" he yelled.

At this point I thought it timely to tell him that my English publisher published from Paris. That seemed to make him hopping mad. An English publisher in Paris! It was a violation of the rules of nature. Well, anyway, what were the names of the books?

"There's only one," I said. "It's called *Tropic of Cancer*."

At this I thought he would throw a fit. I didn't know what had come over him for the moment. Finally he seemed to bring himself under partial control and, in the suavest, the most sarcastic voice imaginable, he said: "Come, Mr. Miller, you don't mean to tell me that you write *medical* books too?"

It was my turn to be flabbergasted. The two of them were standing there boring me through with their mean gimlet-like eyes.

"The *Tropic of Cancer*," I said slowly and solemnly, "is *not* a medical book."

"Well, what is it then?" they asked simultaneously.

"The title," I answered, "is a symbolic title. The Tropic of Cancer is a name given in text-books to a temperate zone lying above the Equator. Below the Equator you have the Tropic of Capricorn, which is the south temperate zone. The book, of course, has nothing to do with climatic conditions either, unless it be a sort of mental climate. Cancer is a name which has always intrigued me: you'll find it in zodiacal lore too. Etymologically it comes from chancre, meaning crab. In Chinese symbolism it is a sign of great importance. The crab is the only living creature which can walk backwards and forwards and sideways with equal facility. Of course my book doesn't treat of all this explicitly. It's a novel, or rather an autobiographical document. If my trunk were here I might have shown you a copy. I think you'd be interested in it. By the way, the reason it was published in Paris is because it's too obscene for England or America. Too much cancer in it, if you know what I mean . . ."

This brought the discussion to a close. The tall slim fellow packed his brief case, put on his hat and coat and waited impatiently for the little fellow to get ready. I asked for my passport again. The tall slim fellow went behind the screen and got it for me. I opened it and I saw that he had drawn a big black X through my visa. That infuriated me. It was like a black mark against my good name. "Where's a place to put up for the night in this burg?" I asked, putting as much snot and venom in it as I could muster.

"The constable here will take care of that," says the big fellow, giving me a wry smile and turning on his heel. And with that I see a very tall man dressed in black with a big helmet and a cadaverous face coming towards me out of the gloom of the far corner.

"What do you mean?" I yelled. "Do you mean that I'm under arrest?"

"No, I wouldn't say *that,* Mr. Miller. The constable will put you up for the night and in the morning he'll put you on the boat for Dieppe." And he started to walk away again.

"O. K." I said. "But you're going to see me back here, maybe next week."

By this time the constable was at my side and had me by the arm. I was white with rage, but that firm grasp of the arm told me it was useless to say anything more. It was like the hand of death itself.

As we walked towards the door I explained very calmly to the constable that my trunk had gone on to London and that it contained all my manuscripts as well as other things.

"We can take care of that, Mr. Miller," he says in a quiet, low, steady voice. "Just step this way with me," and he made for the telegraph office. I gave him the necessary dope and he assured me in his quiet, easy voice that I'd have my things in the morning, the first thing in the morning. I knew from the way he spoke that he was a man of his word. Somehow I had an instant respect for him. I did wish, however, that he'd let go my arm. Shit, I wasn't a criminal, and even if I did want to make a break for it where would I go? I couldn't jump in the sea, could I? However, it was no use starting things with him. He was a man who obeyed orders and it was enough just to take one look at him to know that he had been trained like a dog. He escorted me gently and firmly to the hoosegow. We had to pass through a number of vacant, dim-lit rooms or halls to get to the joint. Each time we opened a door he paused and, taking out a bunch of keys, locked the door behind us. It was impressive. I began to get a bit of a thrill out of it. It was ridiculous and awesome at the same time.

Christ knows what he would have done if I had been a really dangerous criminal. I suppose he'd have manacled me first. Anyway, finally we got to the hoosegow, which was a sort of big gloomy waiting room very dimly lit. There wasn't a soul in the place, nothing but a few long empty benches, as far as I could make out.

"Here's where we spend the night," said the constable in the same quiet, steady voice. Really a gentle voice it was. I was beginning to take a liking to him. "There's a wash room in there," he added, pointing to a door just in back of me.

"I don't need to wash up," I said. "What I'd really like to do is to take a crap."

"You'll find the place in there," he answered, and opening the door he turned on the light for me.

I went in, took my coats off and sat down. Suddenly, as I was sitting there I looked up and to my amazement there was the constable sitting by the doorway on a little stool. I wouldn't say he was watching me, but certainly he had one eye on me, as they say. At once my bowels were paralyzed. *That,* I thought to myself, that beats everything! And then and there I made a mental note to write about the incident.

As I was buttoning up I expressed a little of my amazement. He took what I said in good part, replying very simply that it was part of his duty. "I've got to keep you under observation until I hand you over to the captain in the morning," he said. "Those are the orders."

"Do people try to run away sometimes?" I asked.

"Not very often," he said. "But things are very bad now, you know, and lots of people are trying to get into England who don't belong here. People who are looking for work, you know."

"Yes, I know," I said. "Things are in a mess."

I was pacing slowly up and down in the big waiting room. Suddenly I felt rather chilly. I went over to the big bench where my overcoat was lying and flung it around my shoulders.

"Would you like me to build you a fire, sir?" the constable suddenly asked.

I thought it was damned considerate of him to ask a

question like that and so I said, "Why, I don't know. How about *you?* Do you want a fire too?"

"It isn't that, sir," he said. "You see the law entitles you to a fire, if you wish it."

"The hell with that!" I said. "The question is, would it be a bother to make one? Perhaps I can help you."

"No, it's my duty to make you a fire if you wish it. I have nothing to do but look after you."

"Well, if that's the case, let's have a fire," I said. I sat down on the bench and watched him getting it started. Pretty decent, I thought to myself. So the law entitles you to a fire. Well, I'll be God-damned!

When the fire was made the constable suggested that I stretch out on the bench and make myself comfortable. He dug up a cushion from somewhere and a blanket. I lay there looking at the fire and thinking what a strange world it is after all. I mean how on the one hand they man-handle you and on the other hand they nurse you like a baby. All written down in the same book, like debit and credit columns in a ledger. The government is the invisible bookkeeper who makes the entries, and the constable is just a sort of human blotter who dries the ink. If you happen to get a kick in the ass or a couple of teeth pushed down your throat that's gratis and no record is made of it.

The constable was sitting on the little stool by the fire-side reading the evening paper. He said he would just sit there and read a bit until I fell asleep. He said it in a neighborly way, without the slightest malice or sarcasm. A different species entirely from the other two bastards whom I had just left.

I watched him reading the paper for a while and then I started to talk to him, in a human way, what I mean, not like he was the constable and me the prisoner. He was not an unintelligent man, nor did he lack sensibility. He struck me, in fact, very much like a fine greyhound, something anyway with blood and breeding. Whereas those other two farts, who were also doing their duty by the government, impressed me as a couple of sadistic jakes, as mean, low, cringing bastards who enjoyed doing their dirty work for the government. I'm sure if the constable were to kill a man in the line of duty you could forgive him for it. But those other pimps! Bah! I spat into the fire with disgust.

I was curious to know if the constable ever did any serious reading. To my surprise he told me that he had read Shaw and Belloc and Chesterton—and some of Somerset Maugham's work. *Of Human Bondage* was a great book, he thought. I thought so too and I scored another strike for the constable on my mental blackboard.

"And you're a writer too?" he said, very gently, almost timidly, I thought.

"A bit of a one," I said diffidently. And then impulsively, falteringly, stuttering, I launched into an account of *Tropic of Cancer*. I told him about the streets and the cafes. I told him how I had tried to put it all in the book and whether I had succeeded or not I didn't know. "But it's a *human* book," I said, getting up from the bench and moving very close to him. "And I tell you one thing, constable, you impress me as being very human too. I've enjoyed this evening with you and I want you to know that I have a respect and admiration for you. And if you don't think it's immodest of me why I'd like to send you a copy of my book when I get back to Paris."

He wrote his name and address in my notebook and told me he would read the book with great pleasure. "You're a very interesting man," he said, "and I'm sorry we had to meet under such painful circumstances."

"Well, let's not talk about that," I said. "What do you say we do a wink of sleep now? Eh?"

"Why yes," he said, "you can make yourself comfortable on the bench there. I'll just sit here and doze a bit. By the way," he added, "would you like me to order breakfast for you in the morning?"

I thought to myself well that's a pretty swell guy, about as decent as they make 'em. And with that I closed my eyes and dozed off.

In the morning the constable took me aboard the boat and handed me over to the captain. There were no passengers aboard yet. I waved good-bye to the constable and then I stood at the prow of the boat and took a good look at England. It was one of those quiet, peaceful mornings with a clear sky overhead and the gulls flying. Always, looking at England from the sea, I am impressed by the gentle, peaceful, somnolent quality of the landscape. England comes so gently down to the sea, it's almost touching. Everything seems so still, so civilized. I stood there looking at Newhaven with tears in my eyes. I wondered where the steward lived and whether he was up and eating his breakfast or pottering around the garden. In England every man *ought* to own a garden: it's meant to be that way, you feel it immediately. As I say, it couldn't have been a better day and England couldn't have looked lovelier, more inviting, than she looked at this moment. I thought of the constable again and how he fitted into the landscape. I want him to know, if he ever reads this, how much I regret the fact, seeing how gentle and sensitive he was, that I had to take a crap in front of him. If I had ever dreamed that he was going to sit there and keep an eye on me I would have held it in until we got to sea. I want him to know that. As for the other two bastards, I want to warn them here and now that if ever I encounter them again in this life I am going to spit in their eye. And may the curse of Job be on them for the rest of their lives. May they die in agony in a foreign land!

One of the most beautiful mornings I have ever known. The little village of Newhaven nestling in the white chalk cliffs. The end of the land, where civilization slips quietly into the sea. I stood there in a reverie for a long while, and a profound peace came over me. In such moments it seems that everything that happens to you happens for the best. Standing there quiet and peaceful like that I got to thinking of our own New Haven (Connecticut), where I had gone once to visit a man in jail. He was a man who had worked for me as a messenger and we had become friends. And then one day in a fit of jealousy he had shot his wife and then himself. Fortunately both of them recovered. After they had transferred him from the hospital to the prison I went to see him one day; we had a long talk through the steel mesh. When I left the prison I suddenly remarked how beautiful it was outdoors and, acting on impulse, I went to a beach nearby and took a dip. It was one of the strangest days I ever spent at the ocean. When I dove off the springboard I had a feeling that I was taking leave of the earth forever. I didn't try to drown myself, but

I didn't care a hoot if I were to drown. It felt marvelous to dive off the earth, to leave behind me all that man-made muck which we glorify with the word civilization. Anyway, as I came up and swam around I seemed to be looking at the world with new eyes. Nothing was like it had been before. People looked curiously separate and detached; they were sitting around like seals drying themselves in the sun. What I'm trying to say is that they seemed absolutely devoid of significance. They were just part of the landscape, like the rocks and the trees and the cows in the meadows. How they had ever assumed such a colossal importance on this earth was a mystery to me. I saw them plainly and distinctly as natural objects, as animals or plants. I felt that day that I could commit the most dastardly crime with a clear conscience. A crime without reason. Yes, it was that that I felt strongly: to kill some innocent person without reason.

As soon as the boat turned its nose towards Dieppe my thoughts began to take a different turn. I had never been out of France before and here I was returning in disgrace with that black mark against my visa. What would the French think? Perhaps they would begin to cross-examine me too. What was I doing in France? How did I make my living? Was I taking bread out of the mouths of French workers? Was I apt to become a public charge?

Suddenly I got into a panic. Supposing they refused to let me return to Paris? Supposing they transferred me to another boat and shipped me back to America? I got into a terrible funk. America! To be shipped back to New York and dumped there like a load of rotten apples! No, if they were going to try that stunt I'd jump overboard. I couldn't bear the thought of returning to America. It was Paris I wanted to see again. Never again would I grumble over my lot. It wouldn't matter if I had to live the rest of my life in Paris as a beggar. Better a beggar in Paris than a millionaire in New York!

I rehearsed a marvelous speech, in French, which I intended to make to the officials. It was such an elaborate, melodramatic speech that the crossing of the Channel passed like a dream. I was trying to conjugate a verb in the subjunctive when suddenly I saw the land popping up and the passengers flocking to the rail. Now it's coming, I thought. Brace up, me bucko, and unloose the subjunctives!

I stood apart from the others instinctively, as though not to contaminate them. I didn't know just what the procedure would be in stepping off—whether there'd be an *agent* to meet me or whether somebody would just pounce on me with the grappling hooks as I hit the gangplank. It was all much more simple than my anxiety led me to anticipate. As the boat pulled into the wharf the captain came forward and, grasping me by the arm just as the constable had done, he led me to the rail where I was in plain view of the men ashore. When he had caught the eye of the man on the quay whom he was seeing he raised his left hand aloft with the index finger pointing heavenward and then motioned to me. It was like saying *One!* One head of cabbage to-day! One head of cattle! I was more amazed than ashamed. It was so direct and logical, too, that you could hardly quarrel about it. After all, I was on a boat and the boat was pulling in and I was the man they were looking for and why send a cablegram or telephone when all you need to do is raise your arm and point like that? What could be simpler, less expensive?

When I observed the man whom I was being delivered to my heart sank. He was a big brute of a fellow with black handlebars for moustache and an enormous derby which half crushed his big appetizing ears. Even at long range his hands looked like big hams. And he too was dressed all in black. Clearly things were against me.

Walking down the gangplank I was struggling desperately to recall fragments of the speech which I had rehearsed only a few moments ago. I couldn't remember a blooming phrase. All I kept saying to myself was—"Oui, monsieur, je suis un Américain—mais je ne suis pas un mendiant. Je vous jure, monsieur, je ne suis pas un mendiant."

"Votre passeport, s'il vous plaît"

"Oui, monsieur!"

I knew I was destined to say "Oui, monsieur" over and over again. Each time it came out of me I cursed myself for saying it. But what are you going to do? That's the first thing that's drummed into you when you come to France. *Oui, monsieur! Non, monsieur!* You feel like a cockroach at first. And then you get used to it and you say it unconsciously, and if the other fellow doesn't say it you notice it and you hold it against him. And when you're in trouble that's the first thing that pops out of your mouth. *"Oui, monsieur!"* You say it like an old billy-goat.

Anyway, I had only said it once or twice, because like the constable this chap was also a silent man. His duty consisted, as I happily discovered, in nothing more than escorting me to the office of another official who again demanded my passport and my carte d'identité. Here I was politely asked to sit down. I did so with a great feeling of relief and at the same time, taking a last look at the big brute who had dismissed me, I asked myself—where have I seen that man before?

After the grilling of the night before one great difference made itself felt immediately: *Respect for one's individuality!* I think now that even if he had put me on a boat for America I would have accepted my fate tranquilly. There was an inner order to the language, for one thing. He said nothing capricious, nothing insolent, nothing mean or foul or vindictive. He was talking the language of his people and there was form in it, an inner form which had come out of a deep experience of life. It was all the more striking, this clarity, in comparison with the external chaos in which he moved. In fact, it was almost ridiculous, this disorder which enveloped him. It was not altogether ridiculous, because what inspired it was human, human foibles, human fallibilities. It was a disorder in which you feel at home, which is a purely French disorder. He had, after a few entirely perfunctory questions, left me undisturbed. I still had no idea what my fate was to be, but I knew definitely that whatever his verdict it would not be capricious or malevolent. I sat here in silence observing the way he went about his work. Nothing seemed to work just right, neither the pen, nor the blotter, nor the ink, nor the ruler. It was as though he had just opened the office and I was his first client. But he had had other offices before, thousands of them, and so he was not greatly perturbed if things didn't go smoothly all at once. The important thing, as he had learned, was to get it all down correctly in the proper books. And to have the necessary stamps and seals which were to give the case its legal, orthodox aspect. *Who was I? What had I done? Ça ne me regarde pas!* I could almost hear him saying it to himself. All he had asked me was— where were you born? where do you live in Paris? when did you come to France? With those three facts in his hand he was constructing a beautiful little dossier in my name to which he would finally sign his name with the proper flourish and then affix the stamps with the proper seal. That was his job and he understood it thoroughly.

It took him quite a little while to go about this task, I must admit. But time now was all in my favor. I would have sat there until the next morning quietly watching him if it had been necessary. I felt that he was working in my interest and in the interest of the French people and that our interests were one because clearly we were both intelligent and reasonable and why would either of us want to cause any one any trouble? I suppose he was a man whom the French would call a *quelconque,* which is not quite the same as a nobody in English, because Mr. Anybody or Everybody in France is quite another species from Mr. Nobody in America or England. A *quelconque* is not a nobody in France. He is a man like any other man, but he has a history and a tradition and a race behind him which often makes him more than the so-called Somebodies in other countries. Like this patient little man working on my dossier these men are often shabbily dressed: they look ragged about the edges and sometimes, be it said, they are not very clean either. But they know how to mind their own business, which is a very great deal.

As I say, it took him a little while to transcribe this data from one record to another. There were carbons to be adjusted, receipts to be detached, little labels to be pasted on, and so forth. Meanwhile the pencil had to be sharpened, a new stub had to be inserted in the penholder, the scissors had to be found, and they were found finally in the waste basket, the ink had to be changed, a new blotter dug up . . . there were lots of things to be done. And to complicate matters he discovered at the last minute that my French visa had expired. Perhaps it was out of delicacy

that he merely *suggested* that it would be a good thing if I
were to renew my visa—in case I intended to travel out of
France again, he said. I was only too delighted to fall in
line with the suggestion, feeling at the same time however
that it would be a long time before I would ever think of
leaving France again. I gave my consent more out of
politeness and consideration for his valiant efforts on my
behalf.

When everything had been put in order and my passport
and carte d'identité were safely in my pocket again I very
respectfully suggested that we have a little drink together
at the bar across the way. He very graciously accepted the
invitation and together we sauntered leisurely out to the
bistro opposite the station. He asked me if I liked living
in Paris. A little more exciting than this hole, eh? he
added. We didn't have time for much of a conversation as
the train was due to leave in a few minutes. I thought perhaps at the end he would say—"how did you ever come
to get into such a mess?"—but no, not the slightest allu-
sion to the subject.

We walked back to the quay and as the whistle blew we
shook hands cordially and he wished me a bon voyage. As
I took my seat he was still standing there. He waved his
hand and again he said: "Au revoir, Monsieur Miller, et
bon voyage!" This time the *Monsieur Miller* sounded good
to my ears, and perfectly natural. In fact it sounded so
good and natural that it brought tears to my eyes. Yes, as
the train rolled out of the station I distinctly remember two
big tears rolling down my cheeks and falling on to my
hands. I felt safe again and among human beings. The
"bon voyage" was ringing in my ears. *Bon voyage! Bon
voyage!*

A light drizzle was falling over Picardy. It made the
thatched roofs look invitingly black and the grass a little
greener. Now and then a patch of ocean veered into sight,
to be swallowed up immediately by rolling sand dunes, then
farms and meadows and brooks. A silent, peaceful country-
side where each man minds his own business.

Suddenly I felt so god-damned happy I wanted to stand
up and shout or sing. But all I could think of was *"bon
voyage!"* What a phrase that! All our lives we're knocking

about here and there mumbling that phrase which the French have given us, but do we ever take the *bon voyage?* Do we realize that even when we walk to the bistrot, or to the corner grocer, that it's a voyage from which we may never return? If we keenly felt that, that each time we sailed out of the house we were embarking on a voyage, would it make our lives a little different? While we make the little trip to the corner, or to Dieppe, or to Newhaven, or wherever it may be, the earth too is making her little trip, where nobody knows, not even the astronomers. But all of us, whether we move from here to the corner or from here to China, are making a voyage with our mother the earth, and the earth is moving with the sun and with the sun the other planets too are moving . . . Mars, Mercury, Venus, Neptune, Jupiter, Saturn, Uranus. The whole firmament is moving and with it, if you listen closely, you will hear *"Bon Voyage!" "Bon Voyage!"* And if you get still as a needle and don't ask a lot of foolish questions you will realize that to make a voyage is only an idea, that there is nothing in life but voyage, voyage within voyage, and that death is not the last voyage but the beginning of a new voyage and nobody knows why or whither, but *bon voyage* just the same! I wanted to stand up and sing that in the key of Ut-Mineur. I saw the whole universe like a network of tracks, some deep and invisible like the planetary grooves, and in this vast misty slithering to and fro, in the ghost-like passage from one realm to another, I saw all things animate and inanimate waving to one another, the cockroaches to the cockroaches, the stars to the stars, man to man, and God to God. All aboard for the big trek to nowhere, but *Bon Voyage* just the same! From osmosis to cataclysm, all a vast, silent, and perpetual movement. To stand still within the big crazy movement, to move with the earth however she wobbles, to join up with the cockroaches and the stars and the gods and men, that's voyaging! And out there in space where we are moving, where we leave our invisible tracks, out there is it possible that I hear a faint, sarcastic echo, a slimy, anaemic little English voice asking incredulously—"Come, Mr. Miller, you don't mean to say that you write *medical* books too?" Yes, by Jesus, now I can say it with a clean conscience. Yes, Mr.

Nobody from Newhaven, I *do* write medical books too, marvelous medical books which cure all the ills of time and space. In fact, I am writing now, this very minute, the one great purgative of the human consciousness: *the sense of voyage!*

And just as I imagined I saw the idiot from Newhaven cocking his ear to hear me better a big shadow loomed in front of him and blotted him out. Just as I was about to say to myself—"Where have I seen this face before?"—it dawned on me like a flash. The man with the moustache at Dieppe, that face I had seen somewhere before, I recognized it now: it was the face of Mack Swain! He was The Big Bad Wolf and Charlie was Samson Agonistes. That's all. I just wanted to straighten it out in my mind. *Et bon voyage. Bon voyage à tout le monde!*

Astrological Fricassee

I MET Gerald in the lobby of a theatre during the intermission. I had hardly been presented to him when he asked me what my birth date was.

"December 26th, 1891 . . . 12:30 noon . . . New York City . . . Conjunction of Mars, Uranus and the Moon in the 8th house. Does that help?"

He was delighted. "Then you know something about astrology," he said, beaming at me as if I were a devoted disciple.

Just then a dashing young woman came up and greeted Gerald warmly. Gerald quickly presented us to one another. "December 26th, meet April 4th . . . Capricorn—Aries . . . You should get along beautifully together."

I never got the dashing young woman's name nor she mine. That was utterly unimportant to Gerald. People existed merely to corroborate his celestial theorems. He knew in advance what every one was like—quintessentially, that is. In a way, he was like an X-ray specialist. He looked immediately at your astral skeleton. Where the unobserving saw only a Milky Way, Gerald saw constellations, planets, asteroids, shooting stars, nebulae and so on.

"Don't make any important plans the next few days," he would say. "Just lay low for a while. Yours Mars is squared with your Mercury. It won't do any good to make decisions now. Wait till the moon is full . . . You're inclined to be rather impulsive, aren't you?" And he'd give his victim a sly, inquisitive look, as though to say: "You can't fool me, you know. I see right through you."

There was a lot of handshaking going on in the lobby during that intermission. Every one was introduced by his celestial monniker. There seemed to be a preponderance of Pisces individuals about—tepid, kindly, milk-and-water creatures who were inclined to be pop-eyed and lymphatic. I kept a weather eye open for Scorpios and Leos, especially of the female variety. The Aquarians I gave a wide berth.

In the restaurant later that evening Gerald and I got down to brass tacks. I don't remember what he said he was —perhaps Gemini or Virgo—but in any case he was damned slippery. There was something androgynous about him too. He seemed to be wound up about Libra, Leo and Sagittarius. Now and then he made some periphrastic remarks about Capricorn—cautiously, guardedly, as if he were sprinkling salt on a bird's tail.

He talked a lot about the various bodily organs, as well as the joints, muscles, mucous membranes and other parts of the body. He advised his host, who had recently been run over by a truck, to be careful of his knee-caps next month. The young lady on my left was to watch her kidneys—some nefarious influence was just entering one of the houses which had to do with the kidneys and the ductless glands. I wondered to myself just what sort of astral set-up it was which had given him such a liverish complexion, and why he hadn't done anything about it, perhaps with the aid of the local pharmacist.

By the time I had had three champagne cocktails I was thoroughly confused. I couldn't remember whether he had said the coming week was to be a good one financially or full of broken bones. What's more I didn't give a damn. Any Saturnian influences revealed by my horoscope are more than offset by a benevolent and beneficent Jupiter.

Never once did he mention Venus, I noticed. It was as though he didn't give a shit about one's love life. His forte was accidents, raises in salary, and voyages. The conversation was beginning to taste like a dish of cold scrambled eggs at the Hospital for Joint Diseases. I tried to draw him out about Pluto, because Pluto and her mysterious ways intrigued me more than the other planets, but the subject seemed unpalatable to him; he grew glum, almost morose. What he liked were more mundane queries, such as— "Do you think spaghetti agrees with one of my temperament?" or, "Is exercise good for me at this time?" Or, "What about that job in San Francisco—is this the moment to make a move?" To such questions he always had a ready answer. It was amazing what confidence he possessed. Sometimes, just to make his reply more dramatic, he would close his eyes for a moment to make a rapid survey of the celestial map. He could read the future backwards, yet, in some strange way, like everybody else in the world, he had to buy the morning paper to find out what had happened (during our conversation) on the Russian front. Had the stock market crashed during the night I am certain he would have been none the wiser. When the moon went into eclipse a few weeks later he was on the look-out for quakes and tremblors; fortunately, in some forlorn outpost it was recorded seismographically that there had been a disturbance some five or six thousand miles out in the Pacific. No one suffered, except the monsters of the deep . . .

A week or so later Gerald called me up to invite me to a house-warming. He had promised that I would meet a beautiful Sagittarian with red apple breasts and lips like crushed raspberries. "You're going to be very active soon," said Gerald, as a parting shot. The way he confided this bit of news to me sounded very promising—over the telephone. On reflection, however, I realized that activity in and by itself is meaningless. Ants and bees are active, perpetually active, but where does it get them? Besides, I resented the idea of activity. I was at peace with myself and I wanted to remain that way, at least a little while longer.

It was late afternoon when we drove up to Gerald's house. I had brought two friends along, a Libra and a Sagittarius. Both sides of the street, for the entire length of the

block, were filled with cars, mostly limousines, all sleek and
shiny, and guarded over by liveried chauffeurs who had
already begun to fraternize. Seeing us step out of our Ford
coupe they looked us up and down with a critical eye.

It was a rather pleasant little house Gerald had chosen
for his new abode. Pleasantly neutral, I should say. It could
have been the home of a successful palmist or a 'cellist. The
living room was crowded with people—standing, talking,
sitting, sipping tea, munching biscuits. As we entered,
Gerald dashed forward and began presenting us: Libra—
Gemini . . . Sagittarius—Aquarius . . . Leo—Capricorn,
and so on. It was all a bit like Alice in Wonderland and
Gerald, now that I saw him at close range, was a ringer
for the Red Queen.

When the introductions were finished I stood apart, at
the bay window, and surveyed the scene. I was wondering
who would fasten on me first. I didn't have long to wait.

"Are you iterested in astrology?" said a pale, sunken
individual who had with difficulty extricated himself from
the sofa where he had been crushed between two dowdy
females with oatmeal complexions.

"Only mildly," I said, smiling and shaking his limp hand.

"We're all so fond of Gerald. He's really a wizard, you
know. I don't know what we'd do without him."

An awkward pause, since I had made no response. He
continued: "You're living in Holywood, I suppose Mr. . . .
What was your name again? Mine is Helblinger . . . Julius
Helblinger."

I put out my hand again and said, "Glad to know you,
Mr. Helblinger. No I'm not living here, I'm just visiting."

"You're a lawyer, aren't you?"

"No, I'm a writer."

"A writer—how interesting! Indeed, and what sort of
books do you write, may I ask?"

At this point I was rescued by Gerald, who had been
eavesdropping, and who now joined us all a-flutter.

"You mustn't look at this man's books," said Gerald,
holding his arm up with wrist loose and fingers dangling
like broken splinters. "He's got a very naughty mind,
haven't you December 26th?"

Just then one of the monsters on the sofa tried to rise

to her feet with the aid of a thin, gold-knobbed cane. I saw her fall back like a dead fish and hastened to her side to offer my support. As I did so I noticed her legs which were like two splints. Obviously she had never walked any farther than from her car to the door-step. Her eyes, set in a pasty white face, were like two bird seeds. There wasn't a spark of light in them, unless it was the glint of greed and rapacity. She might have been the twin sister of Carrie Nation done by Grant Wood in a moment of satanic illumination. I could see her on the lawn at Pasadena, where she lived, watering the chrysanthemums with a leaky flower pot. She probably went from the hair-dresser to the numerologist and from the numerologist to the palmist and from the palmist to the tea room where, after the second cup of tea, she probably felt a slight stirring in her bowels and congratulated herself that she no longer needed a laxative every day. For her the supreme joy in life was to be able to have a clean stool, no doubt about it. As I gently yanked her to her feet I could hear her dirty heart ticking away like a rusty Ingersoll.

"You're so kind," she said, trying to wreathe her cast-iron face into a beatific smile. "Dear me, my poor legs seem to be giving way on me. Gerald says it's my Mars in opposition with Saturn. That's my cross, I suppose. What are you—an Aries? No, let me think a minute . . . you're a Gemini, aren't you?"

"Yes," I said, "I'm a Gemini . . . and so is my mother, my sister, too. Curious, isn't it?"

"I should think so," she said, wheezing now from the effort of controlling her giddiness. The blood was running through her veins like mucilage soaking through blotting paper.

"Gerald says I worry too much . . . but what are you going to do when the government eats up all your income? Of course I believe we've got to win the war, but dear me, what will be left for us when it's all over? I'm not getting any younger, that's a certainty. We've only got one car now, and God only knows when they'll take that from us. What do *you* think about the war, young man? Isn't it terrible, all this slaughter that's going on? Heavens only knows if we're safe here. I wouldn't be surprised at all if the Japs

invaded California and took the coast right under our nose.
What do *you* think? You're a very patient listener, I see.
You must forgive me if I prattle on like this. I'm not a
young woman any more. *Well?*"

I didn't say a word. I just smiled at her—perhaps a bit
sadly.

"You're not an alien, are you?" she said, suddenly looking a bit panic-stricken.

"No," I said, "just an American."

"Where are you from—the Middle West?"

"No, New York. That is, I was born there."

"But you don't live there, is that it? I don't blame you,
I think it's a horrid place to live . . . all those foreigners.
I've been out here thirty years. I'd never go back . . .
Oh, Lady Astenbroke! . . . well, it's *so* good to see you
again. When did you arrive? I didn't know that you were
here in California."

I was left holding the crutch, as it were. The old bitch
seemed to have forgotten me completely, though I was still
at her side ready to give support to her tottering frame the
moment she should reel or crumple up. Finally, observing
Lady Astenbroke's somewhat embarrassed glances in my
direction, she moved her rusty hinges and wheeled about
an eighth of an inch, just sufficient to make me aware that
she was cognizant of my presence.

"Lady Astenbroke, allow me to present Mr. . . . I'm so
sorry, what did you tell me your name was again?"

"I never told you," I said flatly. I allowed a due pause
and added: "Himmelweiss . . . August Himmelweiss."

Lady Astenbroke winced visibly at the mention of this
horrible Teutonic name. She held up two icy fingers which
I crunched gleefully with a most unseemly hale and hearty
hand-shake. What annoyed Lady Astenbroke more than
the disgustingly effusive handshake was the insolent way in
which I allowed my eyes to fasten on the three cherries
which were dangling over the brim of her incredible hat.
Only a madwoman of the British upper class could have
discovered such a creation. She stood there like a tipsy
Gainsborough to which Marc Chagall had put the finishing
touches. All that was needed to consolidate the feeling of
Empire was a bunch of asparagus stuck between her de-

flated leathery breasts. Her breasts! Automatically my eyes roved to the place where the breasts should have been. I had a suspicion that she had stuffed some excelsior there at the last moment, perhaps when squeezing the last drop of perfume out of her atomizer. I'm sure she never looked at her private parts, as they say. So disgusting! Always had been . . . If only one didn't have to make water now and then one could forget about it entirely . . .

"Lady Astenbroke is the author of the Winnie Wimple books," the old Pasadena derelict hastened to inform me. I knew I was supposed to look *au courant* at this juncture but somehow I just didn't give a damn whether Lady Astenbroke was a celebrated writer or a champion croquet player. So I said quite calmly and cold-bloodedly:

"I'm sorry to say I never heard of the Winnie Wimple books."

That fell like a bomb.

"Now please, Mr. . . . ."

"Mr. Himmelweiss," I mumbled.

"Please, Mr. Himmelweiss, don't tell us you've never heard of Winnie Wimple. Why, everybody's read the Winnie Wimple books. Where have you been all these years? Dear me, I never heard anything like it."

Said Lady Astenbroke condescendingly: "Mr. Himmelweiss probably reads Thomas Mann and Croce and Unamuno. I don't blame him. I write because I'm bored. I can scarcely read them myself, you know. They're really shockingly simple."

"My dear Lady Astenbroke—how can you say such a thing! Why they're fascinating, your books! Last winter, when I had the gout, I read them all over again . . . every one of them. Such whimsy as you have! Such fantasy! I don't know what we'd do without your Winnie Wimples, really I don't . . . *Oh,* there's Baron Hufnagel. I *must* say a word to him. You'll excuse me, won't you, Lady Astenbroke?" She hobbled off towards the other end of the room, screaming hysterically: "Baron Hufnagel! Baron Hufnagel!"

Lady Astenbroke lowered herself onto the sofa—as if she had a glass ass. I offered to bring her some tea and biscuits but apparently she didn't hear me. She was staring with glassy eyes at a photograph of a lascivious blonde, rather scantily clad, which stood on a little table near her elbow. I edged away from her to find myself rubbing bottoms with a faded actress. I was about to excuse myself when I heard a shrill little laugh, like mica cracking.

"It's only me . . . don't bother," she gurgled. "The Eskimos rub noses . . ." Another little peal of laughter, à la Galli Curci falling downstairs. And then: "I'm November 12th, what are you?"

"December 26th," I said, "all goat and a pair of horns."

"How darling! I don't know what I am—a snake or a centipede. A little of the devil in me and a lot of sex." She gave a lascivious wink with her pale china blue eyes. "I say," and she snuggled up closer, "you don't think you could find me a drink, do you? I've been waiting for that bird" (indicating Gerald) "to offer me something, but I don't think he ever will, do you? Listen, what's going on here? Is some one going to throw a fit, or what? My name's Peggy, by the way. And yours?"

I gave her my real name. "Officially," I said, "I'm known as Himmelweiss." I gave her the horsewink.

"*Officially!*" she echoed. "I don't get it. Officially *what?*"

"Gaga," I said. "You know," and I tapped my head.

"Oh, that's it. You mean they're all screw-balls? I thought as much. Listen, who *is* this guy . . . the guy that runs the joint? What's his game?"

"Horoscopes."

"You mean astrology? Listen, I'm not such a dumb cluck. But what's the racket? What did he round them up for? Is he getting ready to shake 'em down? If he tries to rustle me he's going to get a big surprise."

"I don't think he'll bother you any," I said. "Not that way anyway." I gave her another slippery horsewink.

"I get you. So that's his game!" She made a cool survey of the guests. "Not much competition that way, I'll say. Maybe they're just a blind." She gave a supercilious nod intended to embrace the old hags who surrounded us.

"What's *your* game?" she asked suddenly.

"*My game!* Oh, I write."

"Go on . . . do you mean it? What sort of stuff? History, biology . . . ?"

"Naughty books," I said, trying to blush deeply.

"What kind of naughty book? Naughty-Naughty—or just dirt?"

"Just dirt, I guess."

"You mean—Lady Chatterby, or Chattersley, or whatever the hell it is? Not that swill you don't mean, do you?"

I laughed. "No, not that sort . . . just straight obscenity. You know—duck, chit, kiss, trick, punt, . . ."

"Not so loud! Where do you think you are?" She gave a quick look over her shoulder. "Say, listen, why don't we sit down somewhere and talk this over? What else do you know? This sounds promising. What did you say you were —a goat? What's that—Sagittarius?"

"Capricorn."

"Capricorn! Well, now we're getting somewhere. What did you say your date was? I want to remember that . . . Are all Capricorns like that? Jesus, I thought I was sexy, but maybe I'm going to learn things. Listen, come over here, where nobody can hear you. Now, what did you say you wrote again? Straight what?"

"Straight duck, chit, kiss, trick, punt, . . ."

She looked up at me as though she were going to bless me. She held out her mitt. *"Shake,* partner! You're talking my language. I say, can you embroider that a little—from where you left off? Those were good clean words, the coin of the realm. Can't you reel off a few fancy ones? Go on, try it. I'm beginning to wet my pants. Cripes, imagine finding *you* here. And what's about a little drink, eh? Don't bring me any stale horse-piss. Some Bourbon, if you can find it . . . Wait a minute, don't run just yet. Tell me some more before you go. Begin with duck, you know—like you did before. Only ring some fancy ones in. Maybe you and I'll go places before the night's over. You don't just say the words, do you? That'd be cruel. Come here, I want to whisper something in your ear."

As I bent over I saw Gerald heading straight towards us.

"Shoo this guy away, will you," she whispered. "He looks like a dose of crabs to me."

"What are you two whispering about?" said Gerald, beaming like the heavenly twins.

"Brother, you'd never guess . . . would he?" She gave a

dirty laugh—just a little too loud, I gathered from the expression on Gerald's face.

Gerald bent over, using a *sotto voce:* "It wasn't about sex, was it?"

The woman looked up at him in amazement, almost frightened. "Say, you *are* a mind-reader, aren't you? How the hell did *you* know? You don't read lips, do you?"

"I could read *your* lips even in the dark," said Gerald, giving her a withering glance.

"You're not trying to insult me, I hope? Listen, I know a few tricks myself. Maybe I don't know nothing about astrology, but I've got *your* number."

"Shhhhh!" Gerald put his fingers to his lips. "Not here, my dear. You wouldn't give me away before all these people, would you?"

"Not if you can dig up a drink, I won't. Where do you keep it. I'll get it myself. Just tell me. You weren't brought up on lemonade."

Gerald was just about to whisper in her ear when a ravishing beauty who had just made her entrance pulled him by the coat tails.

"Diana! *You* here? How lovely! I never dreamed that you'd come." He waltzed her off to another corner of the room without bothering to introduce her. Probably congratulating himself on a lucky escape.

"He's a dirty cheap skate," muttered the blonde between her teeth. "He could have told us where he kept it, couldn't he? Pretending to be all wrapped up in Diana. Huh! He'd faint if any one showed him a—you know!—with hair on it."

It was the sort of place you couldn't sit long in without being molested. While Peggy went to the pantry to search for liquor, a Norwegian spinster who was serving tea in the next room advanced on me, leading by the hand a celebrated analyst. He was an Aquarian whose Venus was unaspected. He looked like a dentist who had degenerated into a desert rat. His false teeth shone with a blue flame beneath a ridge of rubber gums. He wore a perpetual smile which by turns indicated satisfaction, dubiety, ecstasy and disgust. The Norwegian woman, who was psychic, watched him reverently, giving significance even to his sighs and grunts. She was a Piscean, it developed, and her veins were filled with the milk of compassion. She wanted all who were suffering to come unto Dr. Blunderbuss. He was really unique, she informed me, after he had taken leave. She compared him first to Paracelsus, then to Pythagoras, and finally to Hermes Trismegistus. That brought us round to the subject of reincarnation. She said she could remember three previous incarnations—in one of them she had been a man. That was during the time of the Pharaohs, before the temple priests had corrupted the ancient wisdom. She was working out her Karma slowly, confident that in another million years or so she would escape from the wheel of birth and death.

"Time is nothing," she murmured, with eyes half-closed. "There is so much to be done . . . so much. Won't you try one of our delicious cookies? I made them myself."

She took me by the hand and led me into the adjoining room where an aged Daughter of the Revolution was pouring tea.

"Mrs. Farquahar," she said, still holding me by the hand, "this gentleman would like to try one of the cookies. We've just had a grand talk with Dr. Blunderbuss, haven't we?" She looked into my eyes with the touching humility of a trained poodle.

"Mrs. Farquahar is terribly psychic," she continued, handing me a delicious cookie and a cup of tea. "She was a great friend of Madame Blavatsky. You've read *The Secret Doctrine*, of course? Of course you have . . . you're one of us, I know."

I noticed that Mrs. Farquahar was looking at me strangely. She wasn't looking into my eyes, either, but sort of slant-wise, from the roots of my hair upward. I thought perhaps Lady Astenbroke might be standing behind me— and the three cherries dangling above my head.

Suddenly Mrs. Farquahar opened her mouth. "What a beautiful aura! *Violet* . . . with a touch of magenta. *Look!*" and she pulled the Norwegian woman to her, made her bend her knees and look at a spot on the wall about three inches above my thinning locks. "Do you see it, Norma? Just squint one eye. Now . . . *there!*"

Norma bent her knees a little more, squinted for all she

was worth, but had to confess she could see nothing.

"Why it's as plain as can be. Any one can see it! Keep looking. It'll come . . ."

By now several old hens were crooking their knees and trying for all they were worth to see the halo which enveloped my cranium. One of them swore she saw it very distinctly—but it turned out that she saw green and black instead of violet and magenta. That irritated Mrs. Farquahar. She began to pour tea furiously, finally spilling a cupful over her lavender dress. Norma was terribly upset by this. She fussed over Mrs. Farquahar like a wet hen.

When Mrs. Farquahar stood up there was a tremendous stain visible. It looked as if she had become excited beyond control. I stood there looking at the stain and instinctively put one hand above my head to bathe it in the violet light of my aura.

Just then a clean-shaven, portly, interior decorator type of homosexual gave me a knowing smile and remarked in a suave, silken tone of voice that my aura was perfectly stunning. "I haven't seen one like it for years," he exclaimed, reaching nonchalantly for a handful of home-made cookies. "Mine is just too disgusting for words . . . at least so they tell me. You must have a beautiful character. My only distinction is that I'm clairaudient. I would so love to be clairvoyant too, wouldn't you—or *are* you? I suppose you *are* . . . it's silly of me to ask. Any one with *your* aura . . ." He made a charming little *moue* and wagged his hips. I thought he was going to wave his hand and shout Yoo-hoo! But he didn't.

"You're an artist, I suppose," I ventured, after this flirtatious exchange.

"I suppose I am," he replied, dropping his eyelashes coyly. "I love to handle beautiful things. And I just loathe figures and all that sort of thing. Of course I've lived abroad most of my life—that helps, don't you think? Have you ever lived in Florence—or Ravenna? Isn't Florence just a darling of a place? I don't know why we had to have a war, do you? It's *so* messy. I do hope the English will spare Ravenna. Those horrible bombs! Ugh! It makes me shudder to think of it . . ."

A woman who had been standing beside us now spoke

up. She said luck had been against her the last seven years, ever since she had had her palm read in Majorca. Fortunately she had put aside a little nest egg for a rainy day—a cool million, it was—she said it without batting an eyelash. Now that she had become an agent things were going a little better. She had just made a place for some one at three thousand a week. A few more like that and she wouldn't have to starve to death. Yes, it was rather pleasant work. After all, one had to have something to do, something to occupy one's mind. It was lots better than sitting home and worrying about what the government would do with your money.

I asked if she were a Seventh Day Adventist by any chance. She smiled with her gold teeth. "No, not any more. I guess I'm just a believer."

"And how did you meet Gerald?" I asked.

"Oh, *Gerald* . . ." and she gave a thrilly-dilly little laugh. "I met him at a boxing match one night. He was sitting with a Hindu nabob or something and I asked him for a light. He asked me if I wasn't a Libra and I told him I didn't know what he was talking about. Then he said—'Weren't you born between the first and the fifth of October?' I told him I was born October first. 'That makes you a Libra,' he said. I was so dumbfounded that I had him do my horoscope. Since then things have been looking up. It seems I was under an eclipse or something. I don't understand it all yet . . . do you? Anyway, it's fascinating, don't you think? Imagine asking some one for a light and being told when you were born! He's terribly brilliant, Gerald. I wouldn't make a move without consulting him first."

"I wonder if you could get me a job in the movies," I said. "This is a good period for me, so Gerald says."

"Are you an actor?" She looked rather surprised.

"No, I'm a writer. I'd make a good hack if I were given a fair break."

"Are you good at dialogue?"

"That's my middle name. Do you want a sample? Look . . . two men are walking down the street. They're walking away from an accident. It's dark and they've lost their way. One of them is over-excited. Dialogue . . .

Excited man: Where do you suppose I could have put those papers?

Calm man: Suppositions are often like random shots on a billiard table without cloth.

Excited man: What? Anyway, if they fall into the wrong hands I'm done for.

Calm man: You're done for anyway . . . I thought we covered all that ages ago.

Excited man: Do you suppose some one could have picked my pockets while we were standing there? Why didn't they take my watch and chain also? How do you explain it?

Calm man: I don't. I neither suppose nor explain. I merely observe.

Excited man: Do you think I ought to phone the police? God, man, we've got to do something.

Calm man: You mean *you* have to do something. I have only to go home and go to sleep. Well, here's where we part. Good-night!

Excited man: You're not going to leave me now, are you? You mean you're going to walk out on me . . . Just like that?

Calm man: I always say exactly what I mean. Good-night and sleep tight!

"I could carry on like that for a half hour. How was it? Pretty bad? All impromptu, of course. If I were putting it down on paper it would sound quite different. I'll give you another sample, if you like . . . Two women, this time. They're waiting for a bus. It's raining and they have no umbrellas . . ."

"Excuse me," said La Libra, "but I've got to go. It was so nice meeting you. I'm sure you'll have no trouble finding a place for yourself in Hollywood."

I was left standing there like a wet umbrella. I wondered if my aura was still showing or if it had become extinguished. Nobody seemed to take a bit of notice any more.

Now that the old ones had bathed their intestines with lukewarm tea they were thinking about getting home for dinner. One by one they gingerly raised themselves from their seats and hobbled slowly towards the door, availing themselves of canes, crutches, umbrellas and golf clubs. Lady Astenbroke was remaining, it appeared. She had fallen into a fascinating conversation with a fat Cuban woman who was dressed in a Butterick pattern of the mutton chop epoch. They were speaking several languages at once, Lady Astenbroke being an accomplished linguist. I was standing behind a rubber plant about two feet away from them, trying to decode this amazing lingo. As the departing ones approached to bid her good-bye, Lady Astenbroke bent forward like a broken hinge and extended her clammy paw which scintillated with jeweled rings. The chauffeurs were crowded round the doorway, ready to proffer an arm to their aged charges. Gerald escorted his patrons in turn to their respective cars. He looked like a distinguished bone-setter who had just pocketed a handsome fee. When the last of the derelicts had vanished he stood on the door-step mopping his brow, took a silver cigarette case from his hip pocket, lit a cork-tipped cigarette and exhaled a thin cloud of smoke through his nostrils. A thin crescent moon was visible low above the horizon. Gerald gazed at it a few moments, took another puff or two, then flung the cigarette away. As he re-entered the house he looked about searchingly. A shade of disappointment was visible in his countenance; apparently the one he was looking for had not arrived. He chewed his lips absent-mindedly. "Oh, foodle!" he seemed to say, and then he made a dash for the kitchen where he probably took a quiet nip all by himself.

Lady Astenbroke was now talking French to the Cuban woman. She was gushing about Juan les Pins, Cannes, Pau and other famous resorts. Evidently she had spent considerable time in the south of France, as well as in Italy, Turkey, Jugoslavia and North Africa. The Cuban woman listened imperturbably, fanning herself the while with a diminutive, ivory-studded fan which could only have been stolen from a museum. The perspiration fell in little drops onto her bosom. Now and then she swabbed the huge crack between her tightly squashed teats with a tiny silk handkerchief. She did it quite casually, never once lowering her eyes. Lady Astenbroke pretended not to notice these unseemly gestures. If she had paused to reflect she would have been horrified. Lady Astenbroke had probably never touched her own breasts since the day they shriveled up.

The Cuban woman was very fat and the chair she was sitting on was very uncomfortable. For one thing, her ass was hanging over the seat of the chair like a piece of limp liver. Occasionally, when Lady Astenbroke's eyes roved wildly about the room, she discreetly scratched her ass with the handle of her little fan. Once she put it down her back, not realizing my proximity, and vigorously poked it up and down. It was obvious that she had lost interest in Lady Astenbroke's disconnected remarks. Her one desire was to get home as soon as possible, rip off her corset, and scratch herself like a mangy dog.

I was amazed, when a dapper little man approached, to hear her present him as her husband. Somehow I had not expected her to own a husband, but there he was in flesh and blood, a monocle in one eye and a pair of butter-colored gloves in his hand. He was an Italian count, so I gathered from the introductions, and his profession was architecture. There was something tremendously alert and pertinacious about him, something of the bird of prey and something of the dandy. Something of the poet also, the kind that walks upside down on the ceiling or swings from the chandelier while pondering a phrase or a cadence. He would have looked more natural in doublet and hose with a big heart pasted over his chest.

With infinite patience, not untinged with malice, he stood behind his wife's chair and waited for her to conclude her séance with Lady Astenbroke. An undefinable asperity gave him the air of a Neapolitan barber waiting for an opportune moment to quickly slit his wife's throat. There was no doubt about it, once they were seated in the car he would pinch her until she was black and blue.

Only about a dozen people were left in the big room now. Mostly Virgos and Geminis, it seemed to me. A torpor had come over them, a gentle torpor induced by the sultry heat and the drone of insects. Gerald was in the bedroom, where the photos of his favorite stars—his clients un-doubtedly—were conspicuously displayed. A rather at-tractive young woman was seated beside him at the writing table. They were going over a horoscope together. I recalled that she had arrived with a handsome young man, who was either her lover or her husband, and that they had separated almost immediately.

The young man, who turned out to be an actor—he was doing Western parts at Universal—had the attractiveness of a man who is just about to go insane. He roved about nervously, flitting from group to group, always hovering on the fringe, listening a few moments, then breaking away like a colt. He was dying to speak to some one, I could see that. But no one gave him a chance. Finally he flung himself on the sofa beside an ugly little woman whom he completely ignored. He looked about disconsolately, ready to explode at the slightest provocation.

Presently a woman with flaming red hair and violet eyes made her entrance; in her wake came a towering young aviator with shoulders like Atlas and the sharp, beak-like features of the air-man. "Hello everybody!" she said, assuming that everybody knew at once who she was. "I'm here, you see . . . Couldn't believe it possible could you? Well, get busy, hand out the compliments . . . I'm all ears," she seemed to say, meanwhile perching herself on the edge of a rickety chair, her back straight as a ramrod, her eyes flashing, her toes quivering with impatience. She had an impeccable English accent which belied the mobility of her features. She might have been Conchita Montenegro—or Loulou Hegoroboru. Anything but a flower of the British Empire. I inquired discreetly who she was. A Brazilian dancer, I was told, who had just burst into the pictures.

A Brazilian peacock would have been more accurate. Vanity, vanity! It was written all over her. She had moved her chair into the very center of the room—to make certain that no one else should monopolize the attention of the torpid assemblage.

"Yes, we took a plane from Rio," she was saying. "I always travel by plane. I suppose it's extravagant, but I'm too impatient. I had to leave the dog with the maid. I think it's stupid, all these silly regulations. I . . ."

I . . . I . . . I . . . I . . . She never seemed to use the second or third person. Even when she referred to the weather she used the first person. She was like a glittering iceberg, the Id completely submerged and about as useful to her as Jonah was to the whale. Her toes twinkled as she spoke. Elegant, polished toes, capable of executing the most intricate figures. The sort of toes that would make one swoon to lick.

What surprised me was the rigidity of her body. Only her head and toes were alive—the rest of her was anaesthetized. It was from the diaphragm of this immobile torso that she threw her voice, a voice which was at once seductive and grating. She said nothing which she had not already said a hundred or a thousand times. She sat there like a rat-catcher, always whistling the same tune, looking bright, gay and alert, but secretly bored to tears, suffocated with ennui. She saw nothing and heard nothing, her mind blank and flawless as stainless steel.

"Yes, I'm a Gemini too," I heard her say, implying by the tone of her voice that the gods had indeed blessed her. "Yes, I'm very dual." I . . . I . . . I . . . I . . . Even in her duality she was just a capital I.

Suddenly Gerald came from the bedroom. "Lolita!" he exclaimed, putting an extra rapturous thrill into his falsetto voice. "How sweet of you! How *gorgeous* you look!" He held her with outstretched arms by the tips of his fingers, as in the ballet, and with fluttering orbs he ravished her from head to foot.

As he was going through this little farce my eye happened to rove and alight upon the woman at the writing table in the bedroom. She had taken a handkerchief from her bag and was drying her eyes. I saw her clasp her hands feverishly and glance imploringly at the ceiling. She seemed utterly distraught.

"My dear Lolita, it was so good of you to come. You came by plane, I suppose? How ducky! You extravagant creature, you! And that lovely hat . . . where *did* you buy it? In Rio, I suppose? You're not running away yet, I hope? I've such wonderful things to tell you. Your Venus is magnificent now."

Lolita didn't seem to be at all surprised by this announcement. She probably knew more about the position of her Venus than Gerald and all the psychopomps of the underworld. Her Venus was right between her legs—and what's more, it was always under control. The only time her love life ever suffered an eclipse was when she had the curse. Even then there were a lot of things one could do without opening or closing the legs.

Now that she was on her feet her body had more animation. There was an effulgence about the hips which was unnoticeable when she was sitting. She used them very much like a flirt uses her eyebrows. She arched them coyly, first one then the other. It was a sort of veiled masturbation, such as boarding-school girls resort to when their hands are otherwise occupied.

She made a few steps toward the bedroom with the sprightliness of an icicle just begining to thaw. Her voice had a different resonance now. It seemed to come from the girdle of Venus; it was lush and curdled, like radishes floating in sour cream.

"When you're through," she said, glancing over his shoulder at the figure in the bedroom, "I'd like to have a word with you."

What it sounded like was: "Get rid of that weepy wretch in there and I'll tell you about my oojie-woojie love life."

"Oh we'll be through in no time," said Gerald, turning his head stiffly in the direction of the bedroom.

"You'd better make it snappy," said Lolita. "I'm going soon." She gave her left hip an imperceptible jerk, as though to say—"I'm warning you. Make it snappy!"

Just then the Brazilian flyer appeared, laden with a tray of sandwiches and some sherry. Lolita pounced on the food rapaciously. The cowboy with the maniacal look in his eye had jumped to his feet and was helping himself manfully. Lady Astenbroke sat in her corner, waiting disdainfully for some one to pass her the platter. Suddenly it seemed as though every one were on the qui vive. The insects stopped buzzing, the heat abated. The general torpor seemed to be evaporating.

It was the moment the cowboy had been waiting for. He had a chance to spout now and he did, in a deep, booming voice which, despite the note of hysteria, had something ingratiating about it. He was one of those neurotic he-men created by the movie studios who loathe their false masculinity. He wanted to tell us about his fears, of which he had a good skinful. He didn't know quite how to begin, that was obvious, but he was determined to make us listen some-how. So, quite as if that had been the subject of conversation all afternoon, he began talking about shrapnel wounds. He wanted to let us know how it felt to be all cut up and bleeding, particularly under a foreign sky, and no hope of being rescued. He was sick of riding wild horses in the chaparral at a hundred and fifty dollars a week. He had been an actor once, back East, and though he hadn't become a celebrity he had at least done without a horse. One felt that he was trying to precipitate a dramatic situation in which he could display his true histrionic powers. One also felt that he was hungry, that perhaps the reason why his wife was closeted with Gerald in the bedroom was to find out when they would eat again. One had the suspicion that the hundred and fifty dollars a week meant every fifth or sixth week, and that between times they chewed horse-leather. Perhaps too his wife had closeted herself with Gerald to learn what had become of her husband's missing virility. A lot of things were dangling in the air, above and beyond those brutal hair-raising descriptions of shrapnel wounds.

He was a most determined, wild-eyed young man—positively Scorpionic. He seemed to be begging our permission to writhe on the carpet, to gnaw Lolita's ankles, to hurl the sherry glass through the window-pane. Something only remotely connected with his profession was eating him up. Probably his status in the draft. Probably the fact that his wife had become pregnant too soon. Probably a lot of things connected with the general catastrophe. Anyway, he was in the dead center of it, whatever it was, and the more he thrashed about the more obfuscated he became. If only some one would gainsay him! If only some one would take exception to his wild, random remarks! But no, no one opened his lips. They sat there, quiet as sheep, and watched him go through his contortions.

At first it was rather difficult to know just where he had oriented himself—amidst the flying shrapnel. He had already mentioned nine different countries without pausing to catch his breath. He had been routed out of Warsaw, bombed out of Rotterdam, driven to the sea at Dunkirk, fallen at Thermopylae, flown to Crete and been rescued by a fishing boat, and now, finally, he was somewhere in the wilds of Australia, grubbing a bite of food from the cannibals of the high plateaus. One couldn't say whether he had actually participated in these bloody disasters or whether he was rehearsing a part for a new radio program. He used all the pronouns, personal, reflexive, possessive, indiscriminately. Sometimes he was piloting a plane, sometimes he was merely a straggler and free-booter in the wake of a defeated army. At one moment he was living on mice and herrings, at another he was swilling champagne like Eric von Stroheim. Under all circumstances, no matter what the time or place he was miserable. Words can't describe how miserable he wanted us to believe he felt.

It was in the midst of this fever and agony that I decided to get up and take a stroll about the grounds. In the driveway leading to the garden I met my Sagittarian friend, Humberto, who had just sneaked away from the clutches of a hunch-backed woman with eczema. We walked back to the garden, where we found a ping-pong table. A young couple, who introduced themselves as brother and sister, invited us to join them in a game of doubles. We had hardly begun to play when the cow-boy made his appearance on the back porch; he watched us in glum silence for a few minutes, then disappeared inside. Presently a very suntanned woman, full of vim and bounce, came out and watched us hungrily. She was like a bull in female clothes, her nostrils breathing fire, her breasts heaving like ripe cantaloupes. The first ball she took a swat at broke in two; the second went over the fence; the third ball caught my friend Humberto square in the eye. With this she retired in disgust, saying that she preferred Badminton.

In a few moments Gerald came out to ask us to stay for dinner. The interior decorator friend had promised to make spaghetti for us, he informed us. "Now don't run away," he said, pointing his finger at us mockingly.

We of course said we wouldn't think of staying. (Couldn't he see that we were bored stiff?)

"Oh, so you don't like spaghetti? It's not good enough for you, is that it?" said Gerald, putting on the pouting hussy act.

"Can we get some wine?" I asked, hoping that he would

take the hint and tell us that cocktails were being prepared.

"Now don't go worrying about those things," said Gerald. "You Capricorns are so damned practical. Yes, we'll have something to drink for you."

"What sort of drink?" said Humberto, whose lips had been parched all afternoon.

"Oh, shush!" said Gerald. "Concentrate on the ping-pong. Haven't you any manners?"

"I'm thirsty," Humberto persisted.

"Then come inside and I'll give you a glass of cold water. That'll do you good. You're getting too excited. Besides, you should watch your liver. Wine is poison for you."

"Offer me something else then," said Humberto, determined to wheedle something alcoholic out of him.

"Now listen, Sagittarius . . . you've got to behave like a gentleman. This isn't John Barrymore's tenement house. Run along now and play your ping-pong. I'm going to send a charming little girl out to play with you." He turned his back on us and slid inside.

"Can you beat that?" said Humberto, throwing his racket aside and pulling on his jacket. "I'm going to get myself a drink." He looked around, waiting for some one to join him. The brother of the beautiful-looking Leo agreed to go along.

"Don't stay too long!" said Humberto's wife.

Humberto suddenly remembered he had forgotten something. He went up to his wife and asked her where her bag was. "I need some change," he said. He fished around in the bag and extracted a couple of bills.

"That means we won't see Humberto for a few hours," said his wife.

They had hardly left when the "charming" young girl came out. She was about sixteen, gawky, with carroty red hair and pimples. Gerald stuck his head out to give an approving nod. Suddenly no one wanted to play any more. The girl was almost on the verge of tears. At this moment, however, the bull-dyker reappeared, rushed to the table and grabbed a racket. "I'll play with you," she said to the gawky one, and with that she whizzed a fast one just over the girl's head. "I've got too much energy," she muttered. She slapped her thighs with the racket while the young gawk crawled on hands and knees among the rose-bushes in search of the ball.

We sat on the stoop and watched them a few minutes. Sister Leo, with the golden spots in her eyes, was talking about the dunes of Indiana. She confided that she had come to California to be near her brother, who was in an army camp nearby. She had found herself a job in a department store, selling candies. "I hope Rodney doesn't get drunk," she murmured. "He can't stand very much. You don't think Humberto will get him drunk, do you?"

We assured her that her brother was in good hands.

"I don't want him to get into trouble," she continued. "When he drinks he's apt to pick up with any one. There's so much disease around here . . . you know what I mean. That's why I like to be near him. I don't mind if he finds a nice, clean girl . . . but those other women . . . I understand all the boys get infected some time or other. Rodney never did run around very much at home. We were always good pals together . . ." She looked at me suddenly and exclaimed: "You're smiling. Did I say something foolish?"

"Oh no," I said, "on the contrary, I thought it was very touching."

"Touching? What do you mean? You don't think Rodney's a sissy, do you?"

"I wasn't thinking of Rodney."

"You think there's something wrong with *me?*"

"No, I don't think there's anything wrong . . ."

"You think I'm in love with him?" She laughed gaily. "Well, if you want to know the truth, I *am* in love with him. If he weren't my brother I'd marry him. Wouldn't you?"

"I don't know," I said, "I never was a sister."

A woman came out on the back porch to put some garbage in the can. She didn't look like a charwoman—there was something "spiritual" about her.

"Don't catch cold sitting out here," said the old lady. "The nights are treacherous, you know. We'll be having dinner for you shortly." She gave us a motherly smile, stood a moment with hands clasped over her fallen womb, and disappeared inside.

"Who is she?" I asked.

"That's my mother," said Miss Leo. "Isn't she sweet?"

"Why yes," I said, somewhat surprised that her mother should be doing Gerald's dirty work.

"She's a Quaker," said the girl. "By the way, you can call me Carol if you like. That's my name. Mother doesn't believe in astrology, but she likes Gerald. She thinks he's helpless."

"Are you a Quaker too?"

"Oh no, I haven't any religion. I'm just a plain country girl. I guess I'm sort of dumb."

"I don't think you're so very dumb," I said.

"Maybe not so very . . . but dumb just the same," she responded.

"How do you know? What gives you that idea?"

"By listening to other people talk. I can tell what I sound like when I open my mouth. You see, I just have simple, ordinary thoughts. Most people are too complicated for me. I listen, but I don't know what they're talking about."

"That sounds most intelligent to me," I confessed. "Tell me, do you dream much?"

She seemed startled by this. "What makes you ask that? How do you know I dream?"

"Why everybody dreams, don't you know that?"

"Yes, I've heard say they do . . . but you didn't mean it that way. Most people forget their dreams, don't they?"

I nodded.

"Well, I don't," said Carol, brightening suddenly. I remember everything, every detail. I have wonderful dreams. Maybe that's why I don't use my mind more. I dream all day long, as well as at night. It's easier, I suppose. Anyway, I'd rather dream than think . . . you know what I mean?"

I pretended to look puzzled.

"Oh, you know what I mean," she continued. "You can think and think and not get anywhere. But when you dream it's always there—whatever you want, just as you want it. It's like a short cut. Maybe that makes your brain soft, but I don't care. I wouldn't change even if I could . . ."

"Listen, Carol," I interrupted, "could you give me an idea what your dreams are like? Can you remember the one you had last night—or the night before, for instance?"

Carol smiled benignly. "Of course I can tell you," she

said. "I'll tell you one I dream over and over . . . Of course, putting it into words spoils it. I can't describe the gorgeous colors I see, or the music I hear. Even if I were a writer, I don't think I could capture it. At least I've never read in a book anything like what I experience. Of course, writers don't go in much for dreams, do they? They're always describing life—or what goes on in people's heads. Maybe they don't dream the way I do. I dream about things that never happen . . . things that *couldn't* happen, I suppose . . . though I don't see why, either. Things happen the way we want them to happen, don't you think? I live so much in my imagination, that's why nothing ever happens to me, I guess. There's nothing I want very much—except to live . . . to go on living forever. That sounds a little foolish, maybe, but I mean it. I don't see any reason why we should die. People die because they want to die—that's what I think. I read somewhere once that life was just a dream. That stuck in my head, because that's exactly what I thought myself. And the more I see of life the more I believe it's true. We're all living the life we dream . . ." She paused a moment to look at me earnestly. "You don't think I'm talking nonsense now, do you? I wouldn't talk to you this way unless I felt that you understood."

I assured her that I was listening most attentively, most sympathetically. Incidentally, she seemed to have grown a hundred times more beautiful. The irises of her eyes had become like veils studded with gold. She was anything but dumb, I reflected, as I waited for her to continue.

"I didn't tell you this, about my dreams, but maybe you've guessed it yourself . . . I often know what's going to happen to those around me. Last night, for instance, I dreamed that I was going to a party, a moonlight party, where I would meet a man who would tell me strange things about myself. There seemed to be a light around his head. He came from a foreign country, but he wasn't a foreigner. He spoke with a soft voice which was very soothing; he had a kind of drawl too—like you."

"What sort of things did you expect to hear about yourself Carol?" I interrupted again. "What sort of strange things?"

She paused a moment, as if pondering her words. Then

she said very frankly and innocently: "I'll tell you what I mean. It isn't about my love for my brother—that's very natural, I believe. Only people with dirty minds think that it's queer to love your own kith and kin . . . No, it wasn't that. It's about the music I hear and the colors I see. There is no earthly music like what I hear in my dreams, nor are the colors like those we see in the sky or in the fields. There is a music out of which all our music comes—and colors come from the same source. They were once one, that's what the man was telling me in my dream. But that was millions of years ago, he said. And when he said that, I knew that he must have understood too. I felt that we had known each other in some other world. But I also knew, from the way he spoke, that it was dangerous to admit such things in public. I had a sudden fear that if I were not careful people would consider me insane and then I would be put away and I would never dream again. I didn't fear that I would go insane—only that by putting me away they would murder this dream life. Then the man said something to me which frightened me. He said: *'But you are insane already, my dear girl. You have nothing to worry about.'* And then he disappeared. The next moment I saw everything in natural colors, only the colors were misplaced. The grass was violet instead of green; horses were blue; men and women were gray, ashen gray, like evil spirits; the sun was black, the moon was green. I knew then that I was out of my mind. I looked for my brother and when I found him he was staring at himself in a mirror. I looked over his shoulder, into the mirror, and I could no longer recognize him. He was a complete stranger. I called him by name, I shook him, but he continued to stare at his image in the mirror. At last I understood that he didn't recognize himself either. My God, I thought, we've both gone insane. The worst of it was, I didn't love him any more. I wanted to run away, but I couldn't. I was paralyzed with fear . . . Then I woke up."

"That's hardly what you'd call a beautiful dream, is it?" I said.

"No," said Carol, "yet it's beautiful to see things upside down some times. I'll never forget how wonderful the grass looked, nor how astonished I was to see the sun so black . . .

Now that I think of it, the stars were shining. They were much closer to the earth than they usually are. Everything stood out brilliantly—much more clearly than in yellow sunlight. Did you ever notice how wonderful things look after a rain . . . especially in the late afternoon when the sun is setting? Supposing the stars were out—and twenty times bigger than we generally see them? Do you see what I mean? Maybe some day, when the earth wanders from its orbit, everything will look like that. Who knows? A million years ago the earth must have had a far different appearance, don't you think? The green was probably greener, and red redder. Everything must have been magnified a thousand times—at least, that's what I imagine. Some people say that we don't see the real sun—only the lens of the sun, so to speak. The real sun is probably so bright that our poor human eyes can't see it. Our eyes are made to see very little really. It's funny but when you close your two eyes and start to dream, you see things so much better, so much clearer, so much lovelier. What eyes are those we see with then? *Where are they?* If one vision is real, why isn't the other also? Are we crazy when we dream? And if we're not crazy when we dream, why shouldn't we dream all the time? Or do you think that's crazy? You see, I told you I was a very simple person. I try to figure things out as best I can myself. But I don't get anywhere trying to think things out. I don't think anybody does."

At this point Humberto and Rodney returned, looking vague and roseate. Gerald was running about frantically, urging his guests to tackle the spaghetti. "It's vile," he whispered in my ear, "but the meat balls are good." We took our plates and sidled up to the Norwegian woman who was dishing it out. It was just like a canteen. The interior decorator went from one to another with a can of grated cheese and sprinkled the cheese over the fresh puke which passed for tomato sauce. He was infinitely pleased with himself, so much so that he forgot to eat. (Or perhaps he had eaten first.) Gerald was hopping about like a cherub, exclaiming: "Isn't it delicious? Did you get a meat ball?" As he passed behind me he nudged me gently and murmured under his breath: "I loathe spaghetti . . . it's vile."

Some newcomers had arrived during the interlude in the garden, youngsters mostly—probably starlets. The one called Claude, with blonde, wavy hair, had a lot of cheek. He seemed to know most every one present, especially the women, who treated him like a pet.

"I thought the party would be over by this time," he said, excusing himself for coming in his pajamas. Then, with a shrill bleat, he yelled across the room: "Gerald! Gerald! I say, Gerald!" (Gerald had just ducked into the kitchen to hide his mortification.) "Oh Gerald! When am I going to get a job? Do you hear me, Gerald? When am I going to work?"

Gerald came out with a frying pan in his hand. "If you don't shut your mouth," he said, going up to the dear brazen little Claude and swinging the frying pan over his head, "I'll crown you with this!"

"But you promised me that I'd have something before the month was up!" shrieked Claude, obviously enjoying Gerald's discomfiture.

"I promised no such thing," Gerald retorted. "I said the chances were good—*if you worked hard*. You're lazy . . . you expect things to come to you. Now be quiet and eat some spaghetti. You're making too much noise." He retreated to the kitchen once more.

Claude jumped to his feet and pursued him into the kitchen. I heard him say—"Oh Geraldine, did I say the wrong thing?" and then his voice was smothered, as if some one had laid a hand over his mouth.

Meanwhile the table in the dining room had been pushed back against the wall and a cute young couple began doing the jitterbug. They had the floor to themselves; every one stood and watched, gasping with admiration. The girl, who was tiny, cute, muscular, energetic, had a sort of Nell Brinkley face à la Clara Bow. Her legs twitched like a frog's under the scalpel. The young man, who couldn't have been more than nineteen, was just too beautiful for words. He was like a faun made of Dresden china, a typical California product destined to become either a crooner or an epicene Tarzan. Claude looked on with veiled contempt. Now and then he ran his fingers through his unruly locks and tossed his head back derisively.

To my astonishment Gerald now came forth and requested Humberto's wife to do a fling with him. He went at it with complete assurance, kicking his heels as if he were cock of the walk. What he lacked in finesse he made up for by his gymnastics. He had his own ideas about the jitterbug capers.

When he got a bit winded he stopped in front of Humberto and said: "Why don't you dance with your wife? She's a marvelous dancer." Now Humberto rarely ever danced with his wife—that was something which belonged to the past. But Gerald was insistent. "You *must* dance with her!" he exclaimed, making Humberto the center of all eyes.

Humberto wheeled off in desultory fashion, barely raising his feet from the ground. He was cursing Gerald for being such an idiot.

Lolita, whom nobody had asked for a dance, was furious. She sailed through the room, stomping her heels, and went straight up to the Brazilian flyer. "It's time to go," she hissed. "Will you take me home?" Not waiting for his assent, she took him by the hand and dragged him out of the room, saying in a loud, cheery voice which was full of ashes, "Good-night everybody! Good-night! Good-night!" (See, this is how I leave you, I, Lolita. I despise you. I'm bored to death. I, the dancer, I am leaving. I will dance only in public. When I dance I leave everybody gasping. I am Lolita. I am wasting time here . . .)

At the door, where Gerald was bidding her adieu, she paused to survey us, to observe if we were sufficiently impressed by her abrupt departure. Nobody was paying any attention to her. She had to do something, something dramatic, to call attention to herself. So she yelled, in her high, stagy, British voice: "Lady Astenbroke! Would you come here a moment, please? I have something to tell you . . ."

Lady Astenbroke, who seemed to be nailed to the armchair, had difficulty in getting to her feet. She had probably never been summoned like that before, but the thrill of hearing her name, the consciousness that all eyes were focused on her, overcame any resentment she may have felt. She moved like a ship in distress, her hat tilted at an absurd angle, her vigorous nose thrust forward like a vulture's beak.

"My dear Lady Astenbroke," Lolita was saying in a voice which seemed to be moderated but which she had thrown to the farthest corner of the house with the skill of a ventriloquist . . . "I do hope you will forgive me for running away so soon. You *will* come to the dress rehearsal, won't you? It's been such a pleasure seeing you again. You *will* come to see me in Rio, won't you? I'm flying back in a few days. Well, good-bye then . . . good-bye! Good-bye everybody!" She gave a little toss of the head for our benefit, as though to say—"Now that you know who I am perhaps you'll behave more gallantly next time. You saw how Lady Astenbroke came trotting to my side. I have only to crook my little finger and the world comes running to me."

Her escort, whose chest was covered with medals, had come and gone without notice. His only chance for fame was to get killed in action. That would increase Lolita's publicity. One could easily visualize the item on the front page. "Daring Brazilian Flyer Killed on the Libyan Front!" A few lines devoted to his exploits as an ace and then a long sob story about his "rumored" fiancée Lolita, the well-known dancer now starring in the big Mitso-Violet-Lufthansa film, "The Rose of the Desert." With photographs, to be sure, revealing Lolita's world-famous thighs. Perhaps in another part of the paper it would also be not too discreetly rumored that Lolita, heart-broken though she was at the news of the Brazilian's tragic death, had her eyes set on another dashing young officer, an artillery man this time. They had been seen together at this place and that during the Brazilian's absence. Lolita seemed to be attracted to tall, broad-shouldered young men who distinguished themselves in the gallant fight for freedom . . . And so on and so forth, until the publicity department of Mitso-Violet-Lufthansa thought the Brazilian's death had been properly exploited. For the next film there would of course be plenty of gossip about. If luck was with them, the artillery officer might also be killed in action. That would provide the opportunity for a double spread . . .

Absentmindedly I had taken a seat on the sofa, along-

side a squat, garrulous creature whom I had been avoid-
ing the whole afternoon.

"My name is Rubiol," she said, turning to me with disgustingly liquescent eyes. *"Mrs.* Rubiol . . ."

Instead of responding with "My name is Miller . . .
Henry Miller," I said: "Rubiol . . . Rubiol . . . where have
I heard that name before?"

Though it was obvious that there could only be one such
name, one such monster in the whole United States, Mrs.
Rubiol beamed with suffocating pleasure.

"Have you ever lived in Venice—or Carlsbad?" she
cooed. "My husband and I always lived abroad—until the
war. You probably heard of *him* . . . he's an inventor. You
know, the triple-toothed bit for drilling . . . petroleum drills,
of course . . ."

I smiled. "The only drills I know of are the ones that
dentists use."

"You're not mechanical-minded, then, are you? Of
course we love everything mechanical. This is the mechanical age."

"Yes," I replied, "I've heard it said before."

"You mean you don't believe it?"

"Oh yes, I believe it. Only I find it rather deplorable. I
loathe everything mechanical."

"Not if you were living with us, you wouldn't. We never
talk of anything else. You should have dinner with us some
evening . . . our dinner parties are always a great success."

I let her rattle on.

"Everybody has to contribute something . . . some new
idea, some fact of general interest . . ."

"How is the food?" I inquired. "Do you have a good
cook? I don't care about the conversation as long as the
food is good."

"What a funny man!" she giggled. "Of course the food is
good."

"That's fine. That's all I ever worry about. What do you
usually serve—fowl, steaks, roasts? I like a good roast beef,
not too well done, and plenty of blood. And I like fresh
fruit . . . not that canned stuff they give you in the restaurants. Can you make a good compôte? *Plums*—that's what

I like . . . What did you say your husband was—an engineer?"

"No, an inventor."

"Oh yes, an inventor. That's a little better. What does he look like? Is he friendly?"

"You'd love him . . . he looks just like you . . . he even talks like you." She rattled on. "He's the most fascinating man when he begins talking about his inventions . . ."

"Do you ever have roast duckling—or pheasant?" I interrupted.

"Of course we do . . . What was I saying? Oh yes, about my husband. When we were in London Churchill invited him to . . ."

"Churchill?" I looked dumb, as though I had never heard the name.

"Yes, Winston Churchill . . . the premier."

"Oh! Yes, I've heard of him."

"This war is going to be won in the air, that's what my husband says. We've got to build more planes. That's why Church . . ."

"I don't know a thing about planes . . . never use them," I interpolated.

"That doesn't matter," said Mrs. Rubiol. "I've only been up in the air three or four times myself. But if . . ."

"Now you take balloons . . . I like them ever so much better. Do you remember Santos Dumont? He took off in a balloon for Nova Scotia from the top of the Eiffel Tower. That must have been very exciting, don't you think? What were you saying about Churchill? Excuse me for interrupting you."

Mrs. Rubiol composed her mouth to make a long, impressive speech about her husband's tête-à-tête with Churchill.

"I'll tell you something," I said, just as she was about to open her mouth, "the dinners I like best are the ones where there's plenty to drink. You know, everybody gets a little drunk, and then there's an argument and somebody gets a crack in the jaw. It isn't good for the digestion to discuss serious things at the dinner table. By the way, do you have to wear a tuxedo at your dinner parties? I haven't got any . . . I just wanted to let you know."

"You can dress as you please . . . *naturally*," said Mrs. Rubiol, still impervious to my interruptions.

"Good! I have only one suit . . . the one I'm wearing. It doesn't look so bad, do you think?"

Mrs. Rubiol gave a gracious, approving smile. "You remind me of Somerset Maugham sometimes," she rattled on. "I met him on the boat coming back from Italy. Such a charming, modest person! Nobody knew that he was Somerset Maugham except myself. He was traveling incognito . . ."

"Did you notice whether he had a club foot?" I asked.

"A club foot?" echoed Mrs. Rubiol, looking stupefactiously gaga.

"Yes, a club foot," I repeated. "Haven't you ever read his famous novel . . . *Of Human* . . ."

"*Of Human Passions!*" exclaimed Mrs. Rubiol, delighted to have guessed the wrong title. "No, but I saw the film. It was terribly morbid, don't you think?"

"Gruesome perhaps, but not morbid," I ventured. "Jolly gruesome."

"I didn't like Annabella so much in that film," said Mrs. Rubiol.

"Neither did I. But Bette Davis wasn't so bad, was she?"

"I don't remember," said Mrs. Rubiol. "What part did she play?"

"She was the switchman's daughter, don't you remember?"

"Why yes, of course I do!" exclaimed Mrs. Rubiol, trying desperately to remember something she had never seen.

"You remember when she fell headlong down the stairs with a tray full of dishes?"

"Yes, yes, of course I do! Yes, now I remember. She *was* wonderful, wasn't she? What a fall that was!"

"You were telling me about Churchill . . ."

"Yes, so I was . . . Now let me think . . . What was it I wanted to tell you . . .?"

"Tell me first of all," I put in, "does he always have a cigar in his mouth? Some people say he goes to sleep with a cigar in his mouth. Anyway, that doesn't matter. I just wondered if he was as stupid in life as he is on the screen."

"What!" shrieked Mrs. Rubiol. *"Churchill stupid?"* Whoever heard of such a thing? He's probably the most brilliant man in England."

"Next to Whitehead, you mean."

"Whitehead?"

"Yes, the man who rang the gong for Gertrude Stein. You know Gertrude Stein, of course? No? Well, then you must have heard of Ernest Hemingway?"

"Oh yes, now I know. She was his first wife, wasn't she?"

"Exactly," I said. "They were married in Pont-Aven and divorced in Avignon. Whitehead doesn't come into the picture yet. He was the guy who invented the phrase 'divine entropy' . . . or was it Eddington? I'm not sure now. Anyway, when Gertrude Stein wrote *Tender Buttons* around 1919, I should think—Hemingway was still sowing his wild oats. You probably recall the Staviski trial—when Loewenstein jumped out of the aeroplane and fell into the North Sea? A lot of water has passed under the bridge since then . . ."

"I must have been in Florence then," said Mrs. Rubiol.

"And I was in Luxembourg. I suppose you've been in Luxembourg, Mrs. Rubiol? No? A charming place. I'll never forget the luncheon I had with the Grand Duchess. Not exactly what you'd call a beauty, the Grand Duchess. A cross between Eleanor Roosevelt and Queen Wilhelmina —you know what I mean? She had the gout at the time . . . But I'm forgetting about Whitehead. Now what was it you were telling me about Churchill again?"

"I'm sure I don't remember any more," said Mrs. Rubiol. "We seem to flit from one thing to another. You're really a very strange conversationalist." She tried to compose her mouth again. "Now tell me a little more about yourself," she continued. "You haven't told me anything about yourself yet."

"Oh, that's easy," I replied. "What would you like to know? I've been married five times, I have three children, two of them normal, I earn about $375.00 a year, I travel a great deal, I never go fishing or hunting, I'm kind to animals, I believe in astrology, magic, telepathy, I take no exercise, I chew my food slowly, I like dirt and flies and disease, I hate aeroplanes and automobiles, I believe in long hours, and so on. Incidentally I was born Dec. 26th, 1891. That makes me a Capricorn with a double hernia. I wore a truss until three years ago. You've heard of Lourdes, the city of miracles, haven't you? Well, it was in Lourdes that I threw away the truss. Not that any miracle happened . . . the damned thing just fell apart and I was too broke to buy another. You see, I was born a Lutheran and Lutherans don't believe in miracles. I saw a lot of crutches at the grotto of St. Bernadette—but no trusses. To tell you the truth, Mrs. Rubiol, hernia is not nearly as bad as people pretend. Especially a *double* hernia. The law of compensation, I suppose. I remember a friend of mine who suffered from hay fever. That's something to worry about. Of course you don't go to Lourdes to cure hay fever. As a matter of fact, there is no known cure for hay fever, did you know that?"

Mrs. Rubiol wagged her head in dismay and astonishment.

"It's much easier," I continued, rippling on like a brook, "to combat leprosy. I suppose you've never been to a leper colony, have you? I spent a day once with the lepers . . . somewhere off the island of Crete it was. I was going to Knossus to see the ruins when I happened to fall in with a doctor from Madagascar. He talked so interestingly about the leper colony that I decided to go along with him. We had a wonderful lunch there—with the lepers. Broiled octopus, if I remember rightly, with okra and onions. A marvelous wine they served there. Looked blue as ink. 'The Leper's Tears,' they called it. I discovered afterwards that there was a lot of cobalt in the soil. Magnesium and mica too. Some of the lepers were very wealthy . . . like the Indians of Oklahoma. Rather cheerful people, too, on the whole, though you could never tell whether they were smiling or weeping, they were so disfigured. There was one American among them, a young fellow from Kalamazoo. His father owned a biscuit factory in Racine. He was a Phi Beta Kappa man—from Princeton. Interested in archaeology, I believe. His hands had rotted away rather quickly, it seems. But he managed pretty well with the stumps. Of course he had a good income and could make himself fairly comfortable. He had married a peasant girl . . . a leper like himself, or a *lepress* . . . I don't know how they call them. She was from Turkey, and didn't understand a word of English. But they were madly in love with one another just the same. They used a deaf and dumb language. All in all, it was a very pleasant day I spent there. The wine was excellent. I don't know whether you've ever tasted octopus. It seems a little rubbery at first, but you soon get used to it. Much better food there than at Atlanta, for instance. I had a meal once in the Penitentiary there . . . it nearly turned my stomach. Naturally the prisoners don't eat as well as the visitors . . . but just the same. No, Atlanta was foul. I think it was fried hominy they gave us—and pork drippings. Just to look at the stuff is enough to make you . . . I mean to turn your stomach. And the coffee! Simply incredible. I don't know how you feel about it, but *I* think that coffee, to be any good, must be black. It ought to look a little greasy too . . . oily like. Everything depends on the roasting, they say . . ."

At this point Mrs. Rubiol thought she would like to smoke another cigarette. It seemed to me that she was looking frantically about in search of some one else to talk to.

"My dear Mrs. Rubiol," I continued, lighting a cigarette for her and almost singeing her lips, "this has been a most delightful conversation. Have you any idea what time it is? I pawned my wrist watch just last week."

"I think it's time for me to go," said Mrs. Rubiol, glancing at her watch.

"Please don't go yet," I begged. "You have no idea how much I've enjoyed talking to you. What was it you were starting to tell me about Churchill when I so rudely interrupted you?"

Again Mrs. Rubiol, easily mollified, began composing her mouth.

"Before you begin," I said, agreeably surprised to see her twitch, "I must tell you one more thing. It's about Whitehead. You remember I mentioned his name a while ago. Well, it's about the theory of divine entropy. Entropy means running down . . . like a clock. The idea is that with time, or *in* time, as the physicists say, everything tends to run down. The question is—will the universe run down . . . and stop? I wonder if you've ever thought of that? Not such an impossible idea, is it? Of course, Spinoza had long ago formulated his own cosmological clock-work, so to speak. Given pantheism, it follows logically that one day everything must come to an end, God included. The Greeks had come to the same conclusion, circa 500 B. C. They had even formulated the idea of eternal recurrence, which is a step beyond Whitehead's theory. You undoubtedly must have run across the idea before. I think it appears in *The Case Against Wagner*. Or perhaps it's in another book. Anyway, Whitehead, being an Englishman of the ruling class, naturally looked with skepticism upon the romantic ideas current in the Nineteenth Century. His tenets, developed in the laboratory, followed *sui generis* upon those of Darwin and Huxley. Some say that, despite the rigorous traditions which hedged him in, there is traceable in his metaphysics the influence of Haeckel—not Hegel, mind you—who was at that time regarded as the Cromwell of morphology. I'm recapitulating all this rather briefly, you understand, merely to refresh your memory . . ." I gave Mrs. Rubiol a penetrating glance which had the effect of making her twitch anew. In fact, I almost feared that she would go into a spasm. I didn't dare to think what I would say next, because I hadn't a thought in my head. I just opened my mouth and continued without a moment's reflection . . .

"There have always been two schools of thought, as you know, about the physical nature of the universe. I could take you back to the atomic theory of Empedocles, by way of corroboration, but that would only lead us afield. What I'm trying to tell you, Mrs. Rubiol, is just this: when Gertrude Stein heard the gong ring and declared Professor Albert Whitehead a genius, she inaugurated a controversy the consequences of which may not be fully felt until another thousand years have elapsed. To repeat, the question which Professor Whitehead posed was this: is the universe a machine which is running down, like an eight day clock, thus involving the inevitable extinction of life everywhere, and not only life but movement, even the movement of electrons—*or,* is this same universe imbued with the principle of regeneration? If the latter, then death has no meaning. And if death has no meaning, then all our metaphysical doctrines are eucharistic and eschatological. And by that I don't mean to embroil you in epistemological subtleties. The trend of the last thirty years is increasingly in the direction indicated by St. Thomas Aquinas. There are no more *pons asinorum* to be traversed, dialectically speaking. We have come out on firm ground . . . *terra firma,* according to Longinus. Hence the increasing interest in cyclical theories . . . witness the battles raging now over the Pluto-Neptune-Uranus transits. I don't wish to give you the impression that I am thoroughly conversant with all these developments . . . not at all! I merely point out that, by a curious spatial parallelism, theories developed in one field, such as astrophysics, for example, produce amazing reverberations in other fields, fields seemingly unrelated, as for example—geomancy and hydrodynamics. You were speaking of the aeroplane a little while ago, of its decisive importance in the ultimate phases of the present war. Quite so. And yet, without a more advanced knowledge of meteorological factors the Flying Fortress, to use a concrete illustration, will only become an impediment in the development of an efficient aerial armada. The Flying Fortress, to make it more clear, Mrs. Rubiol, stands in the same relation to the mechanical bird of the future as the dinosaur stands with regard to the human helicopter. The conquest of the stratosphere is only a step in the development of human aviation. We are merely imitating the birds at present. The birds of prey to be more precise. We build aerial dinosaurs thinking to frighten the field mice. But one has only to think of the hoary ancestry of the cockroach, to give you an absurd example, to see how utterly ineffective was the dinosaur's maniacal development of the skeletal structure. The ant was never frightened out of existence—nor the grasshopper. They are with us to-day as they were with the *pithecanthropus erectus.* And where are the dinosaurs which once roamed the primeval veldt? Frozen deep in the Arctic tundras, as you know . . ."

Mrs. Rubiol, having heard me out to this point, suddenly began to twitch in earnest. Looking past her nose, which had become as blue as a cobra's belly, I saw in the dim light of the dining room what seemed like a bad dream. Dear precious Claude was sitting in Gerald's lap, pouring thimblefuls of some precious elixir down Gerald's parched throat. Gerald was running his fingers through Claude's golden locks. Mrs. Rubiol pretended not to be aware of this dénouement. She had taken out her little mirror and was sedulously powdering her nose.

From the adjoining room Humberto suddenly made his appearance. He had a whiskey bottle in one hand and an empty tumbler in the other. Rocking back and forth on his heels, he looked at us benignly, as if we had requested the benediction.

"Who is that?" asked Mrs. Rubiol, at a loss to remember where she had seen him before.

"Why, don't you remember," I said, "we met at Professor Schoenberg's house last autumn. Humberto is the assistant gynaecologist at the Schizophrenic Sanitarium in New Caledonia."

"Would you like a drink?" said Humberto, staring at Mrs. Rubiol in utter bewilderment.

"Of course she would like a drink. Hand her the bottle!" With this I rose and, seizing the bottle, I pressed it to Mrs. Rubiol's lips. Too fluttered to know what to do, she swallowed a few spoonsful and began to gurgle. Then I put the bottle to my own lips and swallowed a good draught.

"It's getting interesting, don't you think?" I blurted out. "Now we can settle down to a real cosy intimate little chat, can't we?"

Humberto was listening with both ears cocked, the empty tumbler in one hand and the other grasping vainly for the missing bottle. He seemed unconscious of the fact that we had taken the bottle from him. He acted as though his fingers had grown numb; with his free hand he turned his coat collar up.

Spying a cute little vase on the table beside Mrs. Rubiol, I quickly disposed of the wilted flowers and poured a generous portion of whiskey into it. "We'll drink from this," I suggested, "it's much simpler."

"You're a Piscean, aren't you?" said Humberto, lurching violently towards Mrs. Rubiol. "I can tell by your eyes. You don't need to tell me when you were born, just give me the date."

"He means the *place* . . . latitude and longitude. Give him the azimuth too while you're at it; that makes it less complicated."

"Wait a minute," said Humberto, "you're making it embarrassing for her."

"Embarrassing? Nothing could embarass Mrs. Rubiol. Isn't that so, Mrs. Rubiol?"

"Yes," she said meekly.

I lifted the vase to her lips and decanted a half cup of whiskey. In the dining room Gerald and Claude were still playing chick-a-dee. They seemed oblivious of the world. In that eerie light, joined together like the Siamese twins, they reminded me vividly of a water color I had made recently—the one called The Honeymooners.

"You were about to say . . .?" I chirped, looking fixedly at Humberto who had wheeled round and was staring with ice-cold fascination at the Honeymooners.

"Y-e-s," said Humberto, pivoting slowly around, but without taking his eyes from the forbidden sight, "I wanted to ask you if I might have a drink."

"I just poured you one," I said.

"Where?" he asked, looking in the far corner of the room (as if there were a nice clean spittoon there with a cool drink hidden away in it).

"I was just wondering," he continued, "where my wife disappeared to. I hope she didn't take the car." He held out his free hand expectantly, as though certain the bottle would return to its original position without effort on his part. Like a slow motion picture of a man juggling Indian clubs.

"Your wife left long ago," I said. "She went off with the aviator."

"To South America? She must be crazy." By now he had made a few steps forward in the direction of the bottle.

"Don't you think you ought to ask Mrs. Rubiol to have a drink, too?" I said.

He stopped dead. *"A drink?"* he shouted. "She's had

half a gallon already. Or am I seeing things again?"

"My dear fellow, she hasn't had as much as a thimbleful yet. She's been sniffing it, that's all. Here, give me your glass. Let her taste it, at least."

Mechanically he proffered the glass. Just as I was about to grasp it he dropped it and, turning on his heel, staggered towards the kitchen. "There must be more glasses in this house," he muttered thickly, weaving through the dining room as if it were enveloped in a thick fog.

"Naughty, naughty!" came Gerald's voice. "Sagittarius has a perpetual thirst." Pause. Then sharply, like a weary, demented old cluck: "Don't you make a mess in that kitchen, you cute little blunderbuss! The glasses are on the top shelf, left-hand side, towards the back. *Silly archer.* These Sagittarians are always stirring up trouble . . ." Another moment of silence. "In case you want to know, it's now 2:30. The party was over at midnight. Cinderella isn't going to appear to-night."

"What's that?" said Humberto, making his appearance in the doorway with a tray full of glasses.

"I said the party ended hours ago. But you're such an exclusive package we're making an exception for you—and your friends in the next room. That dirty writer friend of yours particularly. He's the queerest Capricorn I've ever met. If he wasn't human I'd say he was a leech."

Mrs. Rubiol looked at me in consternation. "Do you suppose he's going to throw us out?" said her eyes.

"My dear Mrs. Rubiol," I said, putting a judicious tincture of benzoin into my voice, "he doesn't dare to throw us out—it would jeopardize the reputation of the establishment." Then, putting a little edge to the words, "You don't mean to tell me you've finished off that vase?"

I could feel her flustering as she staggered to her feet. "Sit down," said Humberto, pushing her none too gently back onto the couch. He reached for the bottle, or where he thought the bottle was, and began to pour as if it were really in his hand. "You must have a little drink first," he said, almost with a purr.

There were five glasses on the tray, all empty.

"Where are the others?" I said.

"How many do you want? Isn't that enough?" He was

groping blindly under the couch for the bottle.

"How many what?" I said. "I'm talking about people."

"And I'm trying to find the bottle," said Humberto. "The other glasses are on the shelf."

"Don't mind us!" shouted Claude from the dining room.

"Why don't you go home?" shouted Gerald.

"I think," said Mrs. Rubiol, "that we really ought to be going, don't you?" She made no effort to rise.

Humberto was now half-way under the couch. The bottle was standing on the floor beside Mrs. Rubiol.

"What do you suppose he's looking for?" she said. Absentmindedly she took another sip from the vase.

"Turn out the lights when you go," shouted Gerald. "And be sure to take Sagittarius with you. I won't be responsible for him."

Humberto was now trying to raise himself to a standing position—with the couch on his back and Mrs. Rubiol on the couch. In the commotion Mrs. Rubiol spilled some whiskey on the seat of Humberto's trousers.

"Who's peeing on me?" he yelled, making still more frantic gestures to free himself of the couch.

"If anybody's peeing," shouted Gerald, "it must be that Capricorn goat."

Mrs. Rubiol was now holding on to the back of the couch like a shipwrecked mariner.

"Lie flat, Humberto," I urged, "and I'll drag you out."

"What fell on me?" he mumbled forlornly. "This is a hell of a mess." He put his hand on his rear end, wondering, I suppose, if he had dreamed that it was wet. "As long as I didn't make caca . . . Haha! Caca! Wonderful!" he chuckled.

Mrs. Rubiol, who had now righted herself, thought this last was quite funny. She gave a few cackles and then began to choke.

"If you would go to sleep, the lot of you, I wouldn't mind," shouted Gerald. "Don't you have any sense of privacy?"

Humberto had disengaged himself; he was resting on hands and knees and blowing like a whale. Suddenly he spied the bottle. He flattened out like magic and reached for it with two arms, exactly as if he were struggling for a life-saving belt. In doing so he brushed Mrs. Rubiol's shins. *"Please!"* she murmured, her eyes twittering like two desynchronized song birds.

"Please *shit!*" said Humberto. "This is *my* turn."

"Be careful of that rug!" shouted Gerald. "I hope it's not the goat who's in trouble. The toilet is upstairs."

"Really," said Mrs. Rubiol, "this has gone far enough. I'm not accustomed to this language." She paused, as if quite distraught. Looking straight at me, she said: "Won't some one take me home, please?"

"Of course," I responded, "Humberto will drive you home."

"But can he drive—in his condition?"

"He can drive in any condition, as long as there's a steering wheel."

"I wonder," said Mrs. Rubiol, "if it wouldn't be safer if you drove me?"

"I don't drive. I could learn, though," I added quickly, "if you'd show me how the damned thing works."

"Why don't you drive yourself home?" said Humberto, pouring himself another tumblerful.

"I'd have done that long ago," said Mrs. Rubiol, "if I didn't have an artificial leg."

"What?" shouted Humberto. "You mean . . .?"

Mrs. Rubiol didn't have a chance to explain what she meant. "Call the police!" boomed Gerald's voice. "They'll drive you for nothing."

"Fine. Call the police!" echoed Humberto.

"That's an idea," I thought to myself. I was just about to ask where the telephone was when Gerald forestalled me.

"It's in the bedroom, dearies . . . See that you don't knock the lamp over." His voice sounded weary.

"You don't think they'll arrest us?" I heard Mrs. Rubiol saying as I stepped into the next room.

As I lifted the receiver off the hook I suddenly wondered how you ask for the police. "How do you call the police?" I shouted.

"Just yell POLICE!" said Humberto. "They'll hear you."

I called the operator and asked for the police station.

"Is anything wrong?" she asked.

"No, I just want to talk to the lieutenant at the desk."

In a moment I heard a gruff, sleepy voice yelling—*Well?*

"Hello," I said

There was no answer.

"Hello, hello . . . do you hear me?" I shouted.

After a long silence the same gruff voice replied: "Well, what's on your mind? Anybody dead?"

"No, nobody's dead."

"Speak up! What's the matter, are you frightened stiff?"

"No, I'm all right."

"Well, come on then, get it off your chest. What is it, an accident?"

"No, everything's fine. It's just that . . ."

"What do you mean, everything's fine. What are you calling *me* for? What is this?"

"Just a minute. If you'll let me explain . . ."

"All right, all right. Go ahead and explain. But make it snappy. We can't sit on the telephone all night."

"It's like this," I began.

"Listen, cut the preliminaries! What is it? Who's hurt? Did somebody break in?"

"No, no. Nothing like that. Listen, we just wanted to know . . ."

"Oh, I see . . . Wise guy, eh? Just wanted to know what time it is, is that it?"

"No, honest, nothing like that. I'm not kidding you. I'm serious."

"Well, spit it out, then. If you can't talk I'll send the wagon down."

"The wagon? No, don't send the wagon, please. Couldn't you send a car . . . you know, a regular police car . . . with a radio and all that?"

"And soft seats, I suppose? I get you. Sure we can send a nice little car along. What would you like—a Packard or a Rolls Royce?"

"Listen, Chief . . ."

"Don't chief me! Now *you* listen for a change. Shut your

trap, do you hear me? Now listen! How many of you are there?"

"There's just three of us, Chief. We thought . . ."

"Three of you, eh? Now ain't that nice? And I suppose one of you's a lady too. She sprained her ankle, ain't that it? Now listen to me! You want to sleep to-night, don't you? And you don't want any bracelets on your wrists, do you? Well listen! Just go to the bathroom . . . put a nice soft pillow in the bath tub . . . and don't forget the blankets! Then get in the bath tub, the three of you—do you hear me?—and don't let me hear another squawk out of you! Hello! And listen to this . . . when you get nicely settled in the tub, open the cold water faucet and drown yourselves!" Bang!

"Well," yelled Gerald, when I had hung up, "are they coming?"

"I don't think so. They want us to sleep in the bath tub and then fill it with water."

"Have you ever thought of *walking* home? I think a brisk walk would be just the thing for you. Capricorns are usually very nimble on their feet." With this he advanced out of the darkness.

"But Mrs. Rubiol has an artificial leg," I pleaded.

"Let her hop home then."

Mrs. Rubiol was now deeply insulted. She rose to her feet with a surprising alacrity and made straight for the door.

"Don't let her go," said Humberto. "I'll see her home."

"That's right," shouted Gerald, "you see her home like a good boy and then fry yourself a kidney steak. Take the goat along with you." He glared at me in really menacing fashion. Claude now sidled up in his pajama top. Mrs. Rubiol turned her head away.

I had the presentiment then and there that we were going to get the bum's rush.

"Just a minute," said Humberto, still holding the bottle. He glanced towards Mrs. Rubiol disconsolately.

"Well, what now?" snapped Gerald, drawing still closer.

"But Mrs. Rubiol . . ." stammered Humberto, and he looked with pain and bewilderment at her lower limbs.

"I was just thinking," he continued, not knowing just

how to phrase it, "I was wondering, since we're going to walk, if she shouldn't take off . . . well, I mean we could sort of carry her along." He made a helpless gesture with his two hands. The bottle slipped to the floor.

Being on the floor, and not knowing how to express his solicitude in words, Humberto impulsively began to crawl towards Mrs. Rubiol. Suddenly, when within reach of her, he grasped both her legs by the ankles.

"Excuse me," he mumbled, "I just wanted to know which one . . ."

Mrs. Rubiol raised her good leg and shoved him off. Humberto rolled against the leg of a rickety stand, dislodging a marble statuette. Fortunately it fell on the rug; only an arm broken, at the elbow.

"Get him out of here before the house tumbles down!" hissed Gerald. With this he bent over Humberto's prostrate figure and with the aid of Claude raised him to a semi-standing position. "My God, he's made of rubber." He was almost whimpering with rage now.

Humberto slipped to the floor.

"He needs a drink," I said quietly.

"Give him his bottle then and bundle him out of here. This isn't a distillery."

Now the three of us struggled to raise Humberto to his feet. Mrs. Rubiol graciously rescued the bottle and raised it to Humberto's lips.

"I'm hungry," he murmured faintly.

"He wants a sandwich, I guess," I said in a gentle voice.

"And a cigarette," whispered Humberto. "Just a little puff."

"Oh, dragon's britches!" said Claude. "I'll warm the spaghetti."

"No, no spaghetti!" Humberto protested. "Just a meat ball."

"You'll take spaghetti," said Gerald. "I said it wasn't a distillery. It's not a cafeteria either. It *could be* a menagerie, though."

"It must be getting late," said Humberto. "If only Mrs. Rubiol . . ."

"Just forget about Mrs. Rubiol," snapped Gerald. "I'll take Mrs. Rubiol home."

"That's good of you," muttered Humberto. He reflected a moment. "Why the hell didn't you say so in the first place?"

"O, shush! Button your lips! You Sagittarians are just little children."

Suddenly the door-bell rang. The police, undoubtedly. Gerald suddenly became an electric eel. In a jiffy he had hoisted Humberto to a sitting position on the couch. The bottle he kicked under the couch. "Now listen, Capricorn," he said, grabbing me by the lapels, "think fast! This is *your* house and *your* party. You're me, understand? Everything's under control. Some one did telephone, but he left. I'll take care of Claude. Now answer the bell," and he whisked off like a flash.

I opened the door to find a plain clothes man standing there. He seemed in no hurry to rush in and fingerprint us.

"Come in," I said, trying to act as if it were my home and only four in the afternoon.

"Where's the body?" That was the first question out of him.

"There ain't any body," I answered. "We're all alive."

"So I see," he said.

"Let me explain . . ." I stammered feebly.

"Don't bother," he said quietly. "Everything's O. K. I'll sit down, if you don't mind."

As he bent over I suddenly got a whiff of his breath.

"Is that your brother?" he asked, nodding in Humberto's direction.

"No, he's just a roomer."

"A rumor? That's a good name for it. Well, don't I get a drink? I saw the lights and I thought . . ."

"Give him a drink," said Humberto. "And give me one too. I don't want any spaghetti."

"*Spaghetti?*" said the man. "I just want a drink."

"Did you bring a car?" asked Humberto.

"No," said the man. After a pause, in a respectful tone: "Is the body upstairs?"

"There is no body."

"That's funny," said the man. "I was told to fetch the body." He seemed to be in dead earnest.

"Who are you?" I asked. "Who sent you?"

"Didn't you phone for us?" said the man.

"Nobody phoned for you," I said.

"I must have the wrong house. Are you sure nobody died—about an hour ago?"

"Give him a drink," said Humberto, stumbling to his feet. "I want to hear what he has to say."

"Who asked you to come here?" I put in. "Who are you?"

"Give me a drink, like he says, and I'll tell you. We always get a drink first."

"What's this 'we' business?" said Humberto, growing more and more lucid. "Listen, somebody give him a drink, please. And don't forget mc."

"Well," said the man, "you're an astrologer, aren't you?"

"Y-e-s," I said, wondering what next.

"People tell you when they were born, don't they? But nobody can tell you when you're going to die, *right?"*

"Nobody's dying here," said Humberto, his hands twitching for a glass.

"All right," said the man, "I believe you. Anyway, we don't come till they're cold."

"There's that 'we' again. Why don't you tell us? What's your game?" Humberto was almost shouting now.

"I dress 'em," said the man, throwing a bland smile.

"And the others, what do they do?"

"They just sit around and look cheerful."

"Doing what?" I asked.

"Waiting for trade, what do you think?"

Mrs. Rubiol had at last unearthed the bottle. I thought I might as well introduce her. "This is Mrs. Rubiol," I said. "Another body . . . still warm."

"Are you a detective?" said Mrs. Rubiol, extending her hand.

"A detective? What ever gave you that idea?"

Pause.

"Lady, I'm just a plain mortician," said the man. "Somebody phoned and said you wanted us. So I put on my hat and came over. We're just two blocks away, you know."

He got out his wallet and handed her a card. "McAllister & Co. That's us. No frills, no fuss."

"Jesus!" said Humberto. "A mortician, no less. Now I must have a meat ball." He stumbled a few feet towards the dining room. "Hey!" he yelled, "what became of the soubrettes?"

I went to the kitchen. No sign of either of them. I opened the back door and looked out. Everything quiet.

"They've vamoosed," I said. "Now let's see what's left in the larder. I could go some ham and eggs."

"So could I," said Humberto. "Ham and eggs. That's more like it." He paused a moment, as if puzzling something out. "You don't suppose," he whispered, "that we might find another bottle somewhere?"

"Sure, we might," said I. "Turn the place upside down. There must be a gold mine here. Ask the undertaker to help you."

The Brooklyn Bridge

ALL MY LIFE I have felt a great kinship with the madman and the criminal. Practically all my life I have dwelt in big cities; I am unhappy, uneasy, unless I am in a big city. My feeling for Nature is limited to water, mountain and desert. These three form a trine which is more imperative, for me, than any spiritual alimentation. But in the city I am aware of another element which is beyond all these in power of fascination: the labyrinth. To be lost in a strange city is the greatest joy I know; to become oriented is to lose everything. To me the city is crime personified, insanity personified. I feel at home. When, in the movies, for example, I see a great Chinese city, when I imagine myself in the midst of that anarchy and confusion, the tears come to my eyes. It is like a haven for me. No matter what the language I can get along with the man of a big city. We are brothers, we understand each other. Are we not traveling towards a common reality, a reality which had its genesis in crime?

To make the slightest advance one has to go back almost to the very beginning. Every man, when he has earned the rightful death which precedes maturity, returns to his childhood for inspiration and nourishment. It is then that his slumber is disturbed by prophetic, troubling dreams; he resorts to sleep in order to become more vividly awake. Thus he begins to habituate himself, unconsciously no doubt, to the state of annihilation which is earned through fulfilment. He begins to live in full consciousness, in order to enjoy the long, uninterrupted final death, the death which only a very few have experienced. The memory takes on a new character, one almost identical with the waking life. The memory ceases to be an interminable freight train. One consciousness—the same for dream, for memory, for waking life. All motion becomes circular, welling up from an inexhaustible source.

In the violent dreams and visions which accompanied the writing of *Black Spring* one image seems to have recurred with greater splendor and illumination than any other: the Brooklyn Bridge. For me the Brooklyn Bridge served very much as the rainbow did for Lawrence. Only whereas Lawrence was seeking the bright future which the rainbow seemed to promise, I was seeking a link which would bind me to the past. The bridge was for me a means of reinstating myself in the universal stream; it was far more stable and enduring than the rainbow, and it was at the same time destructive of hope and of longing. It enabled me to link the two ancestral streams which were circulating between the poles of death and lunacy. Henceforth I could plant one foot firmly in China and the other in Mexico. I could walk tranquilly between the madman and the criminal. I was securely situated in my time, and yet above it and beyond it.

As far back as I can imagine, my ancestors were straining at the leash. The freaks and monsters which are still to be seen dangling from the family tree are the evidences of a continued violent effort to create new shoots. They were all wanderers, pioneers, explorers, navigators, homesteaders, even the poets and the musicians, even the ridiculous little tailors. On the female side they were Mongols, on the male side they were of Patagonian stock, so it is said. The two streams diverged, leaving traces in every nook and corner of the earth. Finally they commingled and formed the mysterious island of incest described in my book. This island of George Insel was peopled entirely by hippopotamic men, of whom the Atlanteans are one branch. Their peculiarity was to wear nothing but dead men's clothes.

In George Insel the tree and the skeleton became one. The event, which had been hatching for over 25,000 years, took place in a suburban saloon. Suddenly, the exogamists and the endogamists in the family came together—that is, the men who had come down through the Bering Straits as Chinamen encountered in this suburban saloon their brothers from Atlantis, who had walked across the ocean floor during a hippopotamic trance. George Insel came up from the depths like a crater in mid-Pacific. His origins he left behind him. He was straight as a totem pole and clean daft from stem to stern. No sooner had he taken a job as undertaker's assistant than he pounded on a juicy cadaver, evacuated the guts, and appropriated the cerements. When at Christmas-time he peddled postcards, his beard grew very white and sparkled like mica.

Walking back and forth over the Brooklyn Bridge everything became crystal clear to me. Once I cleared the tower and felt myself definitely poised above the river the whole past would click. It held as long as I remained over the water, as long as I looked down into the inky swirl and saw all things upside down. It was only in moments of extreme anguish that I took to the bridge, when, as we say, it seemed that all was lost. Time and again all was lost, irrevocably so. The bridge was the harp of death, the strange winged creature without an eye which held me suspended between the two shores.

I dreamt very violently on the bridge, often so violently that when I awoke I would find myself in Nevada or Mexico or some forgotten place like Imperial City. The feeling I experienced once in the last-named place surpasses description. A sense of desolation truly unprecedented, the more so since it was without cause. I found myself of a

sudden in the body of a man bearing my name in this God-
forsaken spot on the Pacific Coast, and as I walked aim-
lessly from one end of the city to the other I had the very
distinct sensation of not belonging to this body which I
had been made to inhabit. It was decidedly not my body.
It had been loaned to me, perhaps, out of mercy, but it
was not me. It was not terror so much as desolation that I
knew. I who was suffering—where was I in this world at
that moment? There I was conveniently incarcerated in a
body which was walking through a strange city for reasons
I knew not. This lasted a whole afternoon. It was perhaps
the brief period when, according to the astrologers, insanity menaced me. There was no struggle, no great anguish; I was simply stricken desolate. In fact "I" was
absent during the time. The "I" was simply a dim, ap-
proximate awareness of an ego, a consciousness tempo-
rarily held in leash during a crucial planetary conjunction
in which my proper destiny was being worked out for me.
It was the skeleton of an ego, the congealed cloud spirit
of the self.

Not long after that I awoke one night, got dressed automatically, went down to the telegraph office and sent myself a telegram to come home. The next day I was on the
train bound for New York, and when I arrived home the
telegram was waiting for me.

Back in my own skin again I realized without the least
disturbance that I should have to do a long penance. One
does not escape so miraculously without paying a price for
it. A salvation which is earned ahead of time is meaningless. Often on the bridge I had committed suicide. But as
often I was back again, wrestling with the same enigmas.
It does not matter much, in the long calculation, whether
one actually dies or not. One must come back eventually
to live, to live it out to the full, to the last meaningful
dregs. This I came to understand finally when the bridge
ceased to be a thing of stone and steel and became incor-
porated in my consciousness as a symbol.

During the process of inner transformation, the great
current which had animated the family tree for 25,000
years or more became polarized. The terrors and obses-
sions which had eaten it hollow became fixed, death like a

leaven at the base of the tree and lunacy like the air itself enshrouding the foliage. The strange, withered island of incest which was George Insel began to bloom like a magnolia. George Insel began to dream as a plant dreams in a stagnant night. Putting the corpse on the ice, he would lay himself down in the padded coffin of the undertaker's establishment and slowly, drowsily, deliberately dream.

What George Insèl dreamed the men of Mexico dreamed before him. It is a dream which the North Americans are trying to shake off, but which they will never succeed in doing, for the whole continent is doomed. For a time, when the Mongols poured in from the north-west and rented out the uninhabited bodies of the Mexicans, it almost seemed as if the dream were a myth. But to-day, in the angelic countenance of the American assassin, one can see the hippopotamic sleep-walkers who deserted the valley of the Mediterranean in the blind quest for peace. It is in the bland, peaceful smile of the thug, the North American thug, that one can detect the germ of the artist type which was snuffed out at the time of the Flood. What is called history is merely the seismographic chart of the explosions and implosions produced by the aborting of a new and salutary type of man at some definite period in the dim past. This past, as well as the future which will dissolve it, impinges upon the consciousness of the man of to-day relentlessly. The man of to-day is being carried along on the face of his own flood; his most wakeful moments are no different in quality or texture from the stuff of dreams. His life is the foaming crest of a long tidal wave which is about to smash on the shores of an unknown continent. He has swept his own debris before him; he will break clean in one steady accumulated wave.

That is why, in studying the air-conditioned quality of the American nightmare, I am enchanted by the prospect of re-arranging the debris which has accumulated on the shores of that isolated island of incest called George Insel. I see among countless other things a faded flower from Death Valley, a piece of quartz from the Bad Lands, a Navajo bead, a rusty meat-axe from the slaughterhouse, a drop of serum from the Cancer Institute, a louse from a Jew's beard, a street called Myrtle Avenue, a city made

entirely of celluloid, another of cellophane, a cereal like
dried brains called Grape Nuts, and so on. In the dead
center of the debris, thoroughly renovated and thoroughly
ventilated, stands the Brooklyn Bridge. On one tower sits
Tante Melia braiding her hair, on the other George Insel
armed with an undertaker's syringe. The day breaks bright,
and from the yardarms below in the Navy Yard the dead
are swinging stiff and cheerily. Tante Melia is so conveniently situated now that if she desires the moon, as she
sometimes does, she has only to reach for it with her mitt.
Everything is in the best of taste, everything preconceived,
predisposed, predigested, premeditated. The Aurora
Borealis is in full swing and the sky is just one tremendously antiseptic omelette sprinkled with parsley and cara-
way seeds. It has been a fine day for everybody, including
God. No sign of rain, no hint of blood or pestilence. The
weather, like the sky, will continue this way ad infinitum.
Below the river bed some miserable few thousand men are
patiently bursting their lungs with riveting machines.
Otherwise it's quite grand. I walk back and forth over the
bridge with the peaceful smile of the North American
thug. My anguish is trussed up by a permanent elastic
suspensory; should I need to cough up blood there's a
handly little cup attached to my rosary which I bought at
the five and ten cent store once. The battleships are lining
up for target practice; they must be getting into action
soon, or they will be thrown on the dump heap. The rear-
admirals are taking the azimuth; they too are going into
action, like all the other heroes. Everybody will die with
the utmost heroism, including the Grand Dali Lama of
Thibet. Salvador Dali is cleaning his brushes; he feels a bit
antedated. But his day is coming: the air will soon be thick
with placentas, with winged marigolds and spittoons
studded with human eyes. In Yucatan the chicleros are
running amok. Driven to desperation, the Wrigley Brothers
are chewing their own gum. On the shores of the Great
Salt Lake the murdered buffaloes rise up like phantoms
and charge the slaughter-house. And yet the sky is as
bright as an omelette, with every sprig of parsley stoutly
held in place. *A wonderful day for everybody, including
God.*

The North Americans fear two things: death and insanity. In the root type these fears have been banished, seemingly. The killer is a man without nerves and without guilt. He goes about his work in a trance. In the electric chair he displays the same nonchalance as in the barber shop, more in fact, because at the barber's death is apt to come accidentally, whereas the electric chair is a guaranteed paid investment. The man who is sound asleep can be killed over and over again—no pain or terror is involved. But that part of the man which is awake and which at certain periods is denied access to a body creates in time an unseen host which saturates the atmosphere with anguish. Thus the whole continent moves like an icefloe towards some tropical stream in which the tension is to be dissolved.

When I was in it and part of it I had the feeling that the rest of the world was gaga. When a whole continent is drifting there does seem to be direction. But when you stand at the tail end and you suddenly perceive that there is no rudder you get a very different feeling. And if you stand like that for very long you invariably go off the deep end. That is precisely what happened to me. I went off the deep end in a diving suit and cut the hawser. At the very bottom I felt at last that I was standing on solid ground. Looking through the marine depths with aqueous eyes I perceived the soles and heels of those above me who were skating on thin ice. It was exactly as if they were in heaven already, except that angels carry no gatling guns. But they all seemed to wear that blissful expression of those who have passed beyond. They were merely waiting for the scythe to mow them down.

In the act of making the long hippopotamic voyage I discovered a few things which my ancestors had tried without success to din into me. I discovered that one has to breathe very lightly, almost not at all. I discovered that one has to give way, to make painful detours, to swim with the current; I discovered that one must waste a lot of time floating on one's back, that one must cultivate the good graces of the most savage-looking creatures, that one must be absolutely supple and unathletic, a spineless, will-less wisp of the void—if one is to reach the other shore.

The other shore! Above all, one has to learn to forget that there is another shore. For the shore is always there, *when it is necessary.* Just as in the dream the way to avoid extinction is by coming awake, so in the under-water journey the shore is always conveniently there once you decide to lift yourself by the boot-straps. Insanity occurs only when you doubt that you *can* lift yourself by the boot-straps.

The death which awaits us all is the amnesia which inevitably comes to the dreamer who refuses to wake up at the crucial moment. Whole races of men have died off that way, in their sleep, so that death has become pretty much of a habit. And so too it has happened with those who have embarked on the great voyage—those, I mean, who have set out to arrive at the frontier of another reality—that when part of the way across they suddenly lost faith, and with it a foothold in even the flimsiest sort of reality.

The buffaloes which enjoy the longest life are those which are yoked and harnessed. The men who have stopped dying are those who have accepted their fate. The great female principle of surrender produces an equilibrium which keeps the cosmos perpetually cosmogonic and cosmologic. No brick and mortar, no steel girders are required to keep the universe in place, because everything which is is is in its place.

No man who is in a state of grace, which is to say in a state of perfect equilibrium, would want to be a whit different than he is. Behind him, sustaining him like an arch, are the ancestors; before him, receding ever mysteriously into the inferno, are the mothers. He must breathe ever so lightly lest he break through the ancestral membrane which keeps him suspended above the void. He must believe in the miraculous power of his own breath if he would avoid being caught up again in the mill of birth and re-birth. The mothers labor ceaselessly, their loins ever heavy with sordid hopes and doubts. Nothing can arrest the pain of birth unless it be the acceptance of the miraculous nature of one's own being. As long as men deny their own powers the mothers will remain in the service of death.

There are fish which talk and plants which can swallow

alive human beings; there are diamonds which are born in the night during a violent storm. So too there are stars which have not yet moved into our ken and which will announce themselves in good time, without the slightest aid of scientific instruments. When one looks at the thickly studded sky on a clear frosty night one can think two ways, either of which is right, according to one's inner position. One can think *how remote! how unseizable!* And one can also think *how near! how warm! how perfectly comprehensible!* Tante Melia had an obsession for the moon; she was perpetually reaching for it with her two hands. I remember the first time she reached for it, the night she went daft. Never did the moon seem so remote to me. And yet not hopelessly remote! Eternally out of reach, but only so by a hair's breadth, as it were. Some twenty years later I was to see Jupiter one night through a field glass. Jupiter, according to the astrologic lingo, is my benevolent planetary deity. What a remarkable face Jupiter bears! Never have I seen anything so radiant, so bursting with light, so fiery and so cold at the same time. Coming away from my friend's roof that night suddenly all the stars had moved in closer to me. And they have remained thus, some astronomical light leagues closer—and warmer, more radiant, more benevolent. When I look up at the stars now I am aware that they are all inhabited, every one of them, including the so-called dead planets such as our earth. The light which blazes forth from them is the eternal light, the fire of creation. This fire is cold and distant only to those who are looking away from their own warm bowels with crazy instruments of precision.

The book which I speak of was a sort of musical notation in alphabetical language of a new realm of consciousness which I am only now beginning to explore. Since then I have crossed the Equator and made my peace with the Neptunian forces. The whole southern hemisphere lies exposed, waiting to be charted. Here entirely new configurations obtain. The past, though invisible, is not dead. The past trembles like a huge drop of water clinging to the rim of a cold goblet. I stand in the closest proximity to myself in the midst of an open field of light. I describe now only what is known to all men before me and after me standing in similar relationship to themselves. It is impossible for me to say one thing which has not been lived, one thing which is beyond the tips of my hair.

My Mexican incarnation is over, my North American life is past. The thug in me is dead, and the fanatic and the lunatic also.

Mademoiselle Claude

PREVIOUSLY, when I began to write this tale, I set out by saying that Mlle. Claude was a whore. She is a whore, of course, and I'm not trying to deny it, but what I say now is —if Mlle. Claude is a whore then what name shall I find for the other women I know? Somehow the word whore isn't big enough. Mlle. Claude is more than a whore. I don't know what to call her. Maybe just Mlle. Claude. *Soit*.

There was the aunt who waited up for her every night. Frankly, I couldn't swallow that story. Aunt hell! More likely it was her *maquereau*. But then that was nobody's business but her own. . . . Nevertheless, it used to gall me —that pimp waiting up for her, getting ready perhaps to clout her if she didn't come across. And no matter how loving she was (I mean that Claude really knew how to love) there was always in the back of my head the image of that blood-sucking, low-browed bastard who was getting all the gravy. No use kidding yourself about a whore— even when they're most generous and yielding, even if you've slipped them a thousand francs (who would, of course?)—there's always a guy waiting somewhere and what you've had is only a taste. He gets the gravy, be sure of that!

But then, all this, as I afterwards discovered, was just so much wasted emotion. There was no *maquereau*—not in Claude's case. I'm the first *maquereau* Claude has ever had. And I don't call myself a *maquereau* either. Pimp's the word. I'm her pimp now. O. K.

I remember distinctly the first time I brought her to my room,—what an ass I made of myself. Where women are concerned I always make an ass of myself. The trouble is I worship them and women don't want to be worshiped. They want . . . well, anyway, about that first night, believe it or not, I behaved just as if I had never slept with a woman before. I don't understand to this day why it should have been so. But that's how it was.

Before she even attempted to remove her things, I remember, she stood beside the bed looking up at me, waiting for me to do something, I suppose. I was trembling. I had been trembling ever since we left the café. I gave her a peck—on the lips, I think. I don't know—maybe I kissed her brow—I'm just the guy to do that sort of thing . . . with a woman I don't know. Somehow I had the feeling that she was doing me a tremendous favor. Even a whore can make a guy feel that way sometimes. But then, Claude isn't just a whore, as I said.

Before she had even removed her hat she went to the window, closed it, and drew the curtains to. Then she gave me a sort of sidelong look, smiled, and murmured something about getting undressed. While she fooled around with the bidet I went through the business of stripping down. As a matter of fact, I was nervous. I thought perhaps she'd be embarrassed if I watched her, so I fiddled around with the papers on my table, made a few meaningless notes, and threw the cover over the typewriter. When I turned she was standing in her chemise, near the sink, wiping her legs.

"Hurry! Get in bed!" she said. "Warm it up!" And with this she gave herself a few extra dabs.

Everything was so damned natural that I began to lose my uneasiness, my nervousness. I saw that her stockings were rolled down carefully, and from her waist there dangled some sort of harness which she flung presently over the back of the chair.

The room was chilly all right. We snuggled up and lay silently for a while, a long while, warming each other. I had one arm around her neck and with the other I held her close. She kept staring into my eyes with that same expectant look that I had observed when we first entered the room. I began to tremble again. My French was fading away.

I don't remember now whether I told her then and there that I loved her. Probably I did. Anyway, if I did, she probably forgot it immediately. As she was leaving I handed her a copy of *Aphrodite,* which she said she'd never read, and a pair of silk stockings that I had bought for some one else. I could see she liked the stockings.

When I saw her again I had changed my hotel. She looked about in her quick, eager way and saw at a glance that things weren't going so well. She asked very naïvely if I was getting enough to eat.

"You mustn't remain here long," she said. "It's very sad here." Maybe she didn't say *sad,* but that's what she meant, I'm sure.

It was sad all right. The furniture was falling apart, the windowpanes were broken, the carpet was torn and dirty, and there was no running water. The light too was dim, a dim, yellow light that gave the bedspread a gray, mildewed look.

That night, for some reason or other, she pretended to be jealous. "There is somebody else whom you love," she said.

"No, there's nobody else," I answered.

"Kiss me, then," she said, and she clung to me affectionately, her body warm and tingling. I seemed to be swimming in the warmth of her flesh . . . not swimming either, but drowning, drowning in bliss.

Afterwards we talked about Pierre Loti, and about Stamboul. She said she'd like to go to Stamboul some day. I said I'd like to go too. And then suddenly she said—I think this was it—"you're a man with a soul." I didn't try to deny it—I was too happy, I guess. When a whore tells you you've got a soul it means more somehow. Whores don't usually talk about souls.

Then another strange thing happened. She refused to take any money.

"You mustn't think about money," she said. "We are comrades now. And you are very poor. . . ."

She wouldn't let me get out of bed to see her to the landing. She spilled a few cigarettes out of her bag and laid them on the table beside the bed; she put one in my mouth and lit it for me with the little bronze lighter that some one had given her as a gift. She leaned over to kiss me good-night.

I held her arm. "Claude," I said, *"vous êtes presque un ange."*

"Ah non!" she replied, quickly, and there was almost a look of pain in her eyes, or terror.

That *"presque"* was really the undoing of Claude, I do believe. I sensed it almost immediately. And then the letter which I handed her soon after—the best letter I ever wrote in my life, though the French was execrable. We read it together, in the café where we usually met. As I say, the French was atrocious, except for a paragraph or two which I lifted from Paul Valéry. She paused a moment or two when she came to these passages. "Very well expressed!" she exclaimed. "Very well, indeed!" And then she looked at me rather quizzically and passed on. Oh, it wasn' Valéry that got her. Not at all. I could have done without him. No, it was the angel stuff that got her. I had pulled it again—and this time I embroidered it, as subtly and suasively as I knew how. By the time we had reached the end, though, I was feeling pretty uncomfortable. It was pretty cheap, taking advantage of her like that. I don't mean to say that it wasn't sincere, what I wrote, but after that first spontaneous gesture—I don't know, it was just literature. And then, too, it seemed shabbier than ever when, a little later, sitting on the bed together, she insisted on reading it over again, this time calling my attention to the grammatical errors. I became a little impatient with her and she was offended. But she was very happy just the same. She said she'd always keep the letter.

About dawn she slipped out. The aunt again. I was getting reconciled to the aunt business. Besides, if it wasn't an aunt I'd soon know now. Claude wasn't very good at dissembling—and then that angel stuff . . . that sank in deep.

I lay awake thinking about her. She certainly had been swell to me. The *maquereau!* I thought about him, too, but not for long, I wasn't worrying about him any more. Claude—I thought only about her and how I could make

her happy. Spain . . . Capri . . . Stamboul. . . . I could see
her moving languidly in the sunshine, throwing crumbs to
the pigeons or watching them bathe, or else lying back in
a hammock with a book in her hands, a book that I would
recommend to her. Poor kid, she probably had never been
further than Versailles in her life. I could see the expression on her face as we boarded the train, and later, standing beside a fountain somewhere . . . Madrid or Seville. I
could feel her marching beside me, close, always close, because she wouldn't know what to do with herself alone
and even if it was dumb I liked the idea. Better a damned
sight than having some god-damned flapper with you,
some lightheaded little bastard who's always figuring out
a way of ditching you even when she's lying with you.
No, I could feel sure of Claude. Later it might get tiresome
—later . . . later. I was glad I had picked a whore. *A
faithful whore!* Jesus, I know people who'd laugh like hell
if I ever said that.

I was planning it all out in detail: the places we'd stop
at, the clothes she'd wear, what we'd talk about . . . everything . . . everything. She was Catholic, I supposed, but
that didn't matter a damn to me. In fact, I rather liked
it. It was lots better going to church to hear mass than to
study architecture and all that crap. If she wanted, I'd
become a Catholic too . . . what the hell! I'd do anything
she asked me to—if it gave her a kick. I began to wonder
if she had a kid somewhere, as most of them have. Imagine, Claude's kid! Why I'd love that kid more than if it
were my own. Yes, she must have a kid, Claude—I'm going to see about it. There'd be times, I knew, when we'd
have a big room with a balcony, a room looking out on
a river, and flowers on the windowsill and birds singing.
(I could see myself coming back with a birdcage on my
arm. O. K. So long as it made her happy!) But the river
—there must be rivers once in a while. I'm nuts about
rivers. Once, in Rotterdam, I remember — — —. The
idea, though, of waking up in the morning, the sun streaming in the windows and a good, faithful whore beside you
who loves you, who loves the guts out of you, the birds
singing and the table all spread, and while she's washing
up and combing her hair all the men she's been with and

now you, just you, and barges going by, masts and hulls, the whole damned current of life flowing through you, through her, through all the guys before you and maybe after, the flowers and the birds and the sun streaming in and the fragrance of it choking you, annihilating you. O Christ! Give me a whore always, all the time!

I've asked Claude to live with me and she's refused. This is a blow. I know it's not because I'm poor—Claude knows all about my finances, about the book I'm writing, etc. No, there must be some other, deeper reason. But she won't come out with it.

And then there's another thing—I've begun to act like a saint. I take long walks alone, and what I'm writing now has nothing to do with my book. It seems as if I were alone in the universe, that my life is complete and separate, like a statue's. I have even forgotten the name of my creator. And I feel as if all my actions are inspired, as if I were meant to do nothing but good in this world. I ask for nobody's approval.

I refuse to take any charity from Claude any more. I keep track of everything I owe her. She looks sad these days, Claude. Sometimes, when I pass her on the *terrasse,* I could swear that there are tears in her eyes. She's in love with me now, I know it. She loves me desperately. For hours and hours she sits there on the *terrasse*. I go with her sometimes because I can't bear to see her miserable, to see her waiting, waiting, waiting. . . . I have even spoken to some of my friends about her, tipped them off, as it were. Yes, anything is better than to see Claude sitting there waiting, waiting. What does she think about when she sits there all by herself?

I wonder what she would say if I walked up to her one day and slipped her a thousand franc note. Just walk up to her, when she's got that melancholy look in her eyes, and say: *"Voici quelque chose que j'ai oublié l'autre jour."* Sometimes, when we lie together and there comes those long brimming silences, she says to me: *"Que pensez-vous maintenant?"* And I always answer *"Rien!"* But what I'm really thinking to myself is—*"Voici quelque chose que. . . ."* This is the beautiful part of *l'amour à credit*.

When she takes leave of me the bells ring out wildly.

She makes everything so right inside me. I lie back on the pillow and luxuriously enjoy the weak cigarette which she has left for me. I don't have to stir for a thing. If I had a plate in my mouth I'm sure she wouldn't forget to put it in the tumbler on the table beside my bed, together with the matches and the alarm clock and all the other junk. My trousers are carefully folded and my hat and coat are hanging on a peg near the door. Everything in its place. Marvelous! When you get a whore you get a jewel. . . .

And the best of it is, the fine feeling endures. A mystic feeling it is, and to become mystic is to feel the unity of life. I don't care particularly any more whether I am a saint or not. A saint struggles too much. I impart good, peace, serenity. I am getting more and more customers for Claude and she no longer has that sad look in her eyes when I pass her. We eat together most every day. She insists on taking me to expensive places, and I no longer demur. I enjoy every phase of life—the expensive places as well as the inexpensive places. If it makes Claude happy — — —.

Pourtant je pense à quelque chose. A little thing, to be sure, but lately it has grown more and more important in my mind. The first time I said nothing about it. An unwonted touch of delicacy, I thought to myself. Charming, in fact. The second time—was it delicacy, or just carelessness? However, *rien à dire*. Between the second and third times I was unfaithful, so to speak. Yes, I was up on the *Grands Boulevards* one night, a little tight. After running the gauntlet all the way from the Place de la République to *Le Matin,* a big, scabby buzzard whom I ordinarily wouldn't have pissed on grabbed me off. A droll affair. Visitors knocking at our door every few minutes. Poor little ex-Folies girls who begged the kind monsieur to give them a little tip—thirty francs or so. For what, pray? *Pour rien*.......*pour le plaisir*. A very strange, and funny night. A day or so later irritation. Worries. Hurried trip to the American Hospital. Visions of Ehrlich and his black cigars. Nothing wrong, however. Just worry.

When I broach the subject to Claude she looks at me in astonishment. "I know you have every confidence in me,

Claude, but . . ." Claude refuses to waste time on such a subject. A man who would consciously, deliberately give a woman a disease is a criminal. That's how Claude looks upon it. *"C'est vrai, n'est-ce pas?"* she asks. It's *vrai* all right. However. . . . But the subject is closed. Any man who would do that is a criminal.

Every morning now, when I take my paraffin oil—I always take it with an orange—I get to thinking about these criminals who give women diseases. The paraffin oil makes the spoon very sticky. It is necessary to wash it well. I wash the knife and the spoon very carefully. I do everything carefully—it is my nature. After I have washed my face I look at the towel. The patron never gives out more than three towels a week; by Tuesday they are all soiled. I dry the knife and the spoon with a towel; for my face I use the bedspread. I don't rub my face—I pat it gently with the edges of the bedspread, near the feet.

The Rue Hippolyte Mandron looks vile to me. I detest all the dirty, narrow, crooked streets with romantic names hereabouts. Paris looks to me like a big, ugly chancre. The streets are gangrened. Everybody has it—if it isn't clap it's syphilis. All Europe is diseased, and it's France who's made it diseased. This is what comes of admiring Voltaire and Rabelais! I should have gone to Moscow, as I intended. Even if there are no Sundays in Russia, what difference does it make? Sunday is like any other day now, only the streets are more crowded, more victims walking about contaminating one another.

Mind you, it's not Claude I'm raving against. Claude is a jewel, *un ange,* and no *presque* about it. There's the bird-cage hanging outside the window, and flowers too—though it ain't Madrid or Seville, no fountains, no pigeons. No, it's the clinic every day. She goes in one door and I in the other. No more expensive restaurants. Go to the movies every night and try to stop squirming. Can't bear the sight of the Dôme or the Coupole any more. These bastards sitting around on the *terrasse,* looking so clean and healthy with their coats of tan, their starched shirts and their eau-de-cologne. It wasn't entirely Claude's fault. I tried to warn her about these suave looking bastards. She was so damned confident of herself—the injections

and all that business. And then, any man who would. . . .
Well, that's just how it happened. Living with a whore—
even the best whore in the world—isn't a bed of roses. It
isn't the numbers of men, though that too gets under your
skin sometimes, it's the everlasting sanitation, the precau-
tions, the irrigations, the examinations, the worry, the
dread. And then, in spite of it all — — —. I told Claude
. . . . I told her repeatedly—"watch out for the swell
guys!"

No, I blame myself for everything that's happened. Not
content with being a saint I had to prove that I was a
saint. Once a man realizes that he's a saint he should stop
there. Trying to pull the saint on a little whore is like
climbing into heaven by the back stairs. When she cuddles
up to me—she loves me now more than ever—it seems to
me that I'm just some damned microbe that's wormed its
way into her soul. I feel that even if I am living with an
angel I ought to try to make a man of myself. We ought
to get out of this filthy hole and live somewhere in the
sunshine, a room with a balcony overlooking a river, birds,
flowers, life streaming by, just she and me and nothing
else.

Poros Harbor

from "The Colossus of Maroussi"

I AM in Athens. Winter is coming on. People are asking
me—have you been to Delphi, have you been to Santorini,
have you been to Lesbos or Samos or Poros? I have been
practically nowhere, except back and forth to Corfu. One
day I had been as far as Mandra, which is past Eleusis on
the way to Megara. Fortunately the road was blocked and
we had to turn back. I say fortunately because on that day,
if we had gone another few miles, I would have lost my
head completely. In another way I was doing a great deal

of traveling; people came to me at the cafés and poured out their journeys to me; the captain was always returning from a new trajectory; Seferis was always writing a new poem which went back deep into the past and forward as far as the seventh root race; Katsimbalis would take me on his monologues to Mt. Athos, to Pelion and Ossa, to Leonidion and Monemvasia; Durrell would set my mind whirling with Pythagorean adventures; a little Welshman, just back from Persia, would drag me over the high plateaus and deposit me in Samarkand where I would meet the headless horseman called Death. All the Englishmen I met were always coming back from somewhere, some island, some monastery, some ancient ruin, some place of mystery. I was so bewildered by all the opportunities lying before me that I was paralyzed.

Then one day Seferis and Katsimbalis introduced me to the painter Ghika. I saw a new Greece, the quintessential Greece which the artist had abstracted from the muck and confusion of time, of place, of history. I got a bifocal slant on this world which was now making me giddy with names, dates, legends. Ghika has placed himself in the center of all time, in that self-perpetuating Greece which has no borders, no limits, no age. Ghika's canvases are as fresh and clean, as pure and naked of all pretense, as the sea and light which bathes the dazzling islands. Ghika is a seeker after light and truth: his paintings go beyond the Greek world. It was Ghika's painting which roused me from my bedazzled stupor.

A week or so later we all boarded the boat at Peiraeus to go to Hydra where Ghika had his ancestral home. Sefris and Katsimbalis were jubilant: they had not had a holiday in ages. It was late fall, which means that the weather was beautifully mild. Towards noon we came within sight of the island of Poros. We had been having a bite on deck—one of those impromptu meals which Katsimbalis loves to put away at any hour of the day or night, when he is in good fettle. I suppose I'll never again experience the warmth of affection which surrounded me that morning as we embarked on our journey. Everybody was talking at once, the wine was flowing, the food was being replenished, the sun which had been veiled came out strong, the boat was rocking gently, the war was on but forgotten, the sea was there but the shore too, the goats were clambering about, the lemon groves were in sight and the madness which is in their fragrance had already seized us and drawn us tightly together in a frenzy of self-surrender.

I don't know which affected me more deeply—the story of the lemon groves just opposite us or the sight of Poros itself when suddenly I realized that we were sailing through the streets. If there is one dream which I like above all others it is that of sailing on land. Coming into Poros gives the illusion of the deep dream. Suddenly the land converges on all sides and the boat is squeezed into a narrow strait from which there seems to be no egress. The men and women of Poros are hanging out of the windows, just above your head. You pull in right under their friendly nostrils, as though for a shave and haircut en route.

The loungers on the quay are walking with the same speed as the boat; they can walk faster than the boat if they choose to quicken their pace. The island revolves in cubistic planes, one of walls and windows, one of rocks and goats, one of stiff-blown trees and shrubs, and so on. Yonder, where the mainland curves like a whip, lie the wild lemon groves and there in the spring young and old go mad from the fragrance of sap and blossom. You enter the harbor of Poros swaying and swirling, a gentle idiot tossed about amidst masts and nets in a world which only the painter knows and which he has made live again because like you, when he first saw this world, he was drunk and happy and carefree.

To sail slowly through the streets of Poros is to recapture the joy of passing through the neck of the womb. It is a joy almost too deep to be remembered. It is a kind of numb idiot's delight which produces legends such as that of the birth of an island out of a foundering ship. The ship, the passage, the revolving walls, the gentle undulating tremor, the green snakelike curve of the shore, the beards hanging down over your scalp from the inhabitants suspended above you, all these and the palpitant breath of friendship, sympathy, guidance, envelop and entrance you

until you are blown out like a star fulfilled and your heart
with its molten smithereens scattered far and wide.

It is now, as I write this, just about the same time of
day some few months later. The clock and the calendar
say so, at any rate. In point of truth it is aeons since I
passed through that narrow strait. It will never happen
again. Ordinarily I would be sad at the thought, but I
am not now. There is every reason to be sad at this moment: all the premonitions which I have had for ten years
are coming true. This is one of the lowest moments in the
history of the human race. There is no sign of hope on
the horizon. The whole world is involved in slaughter and
bloodshed. I repeat—*I am not sad*. Let the world have its
bath of blood—I will cling to Poros.

Millions of years may pass and I may come back again
and again on one planet or another, as human, as devil,
as archangel (I care not how, which, what, or when), but
my feet will never leave that boat, my eyes will never close
on that scene, my friends will never disappear. That was
a moment which endures, which survives world wars,
which outlasts the life of the planet Earth itself. If I
should ever attain the fulfillment which the Buddhists
speak of, if I should ever have the choice of attaining
Nirvana or remaining behind to watch over and guide
those to come, I say now let me remain behind, let me
hover as a gentle spirit above the roofs of Poros and look
down upon the voyager with a smile of peace and good
cheer. I can see the whole human race straining through
the neck of the bottle here, searching for egress into the
world of light and beauty. May they come, may they dis-
embark, may they stay and rest awhile in peace.

Other SIGNET Books You Will Enjoy

THE BLACK PRINCE AND OTHER STORIES
                                    by Shirley Ann Grau
> An exciting collection of stories of one of today's most
> talented young writers.   (#S1318—35¢)

THE GRASS HARP AND A TREE OF NIGHT
AND OTHER STORIES   **by Truman Capote**
> Two brilliant books in one: an enchanting novel of small
> town people rebelling against their humdrum life, plus a
> haunting short-story collection.   (#S1333—35¢)

STUDS LONIGAN   **by James T. Farrell**
> Three books in one complete, unabridged volume; *Young
> Lonigan, The Young Manhood of Studs Lonigan,* and
> *Judgment Day.* A modern classic.   (#T1518—75¢)

ROMAN TALES   **by Alberto Moravia**
> Stories of the exuberant life in the back streets of Rome,
> by Italy's greatest living writer.   (#S1612—35¢)

A THIRSTY EVIL   **by Gore Vidal**
> Stories that probe the effects of love and lust on confused
> human hearts.   (#S1535—35¢)

SUMMER IN SALANDAR   **by H. E. Bates**
> Four novelle dealing with human love in all its contra-
> dictions, variety, squalor, and passion. (#S1602—35¢)

SATURDAY NIGHT   **by James T. Farrell**
> Vividly etched stories of young people in large cities, told
> with penetrating insight and sympathy. (#S1624—35¢)

TO OUR READERS: We welcome your request for our free
catalog of SIGNET and MENTOR BOOKS. If your dealer does
not have the books you want, you may order them by mail,
enclosing the list price plus 5¢ a copy to cover mailing. The
New American Library of World Literature, Inc., P. O. Box
2310, Grand Central Station, New York 17, N. Y.